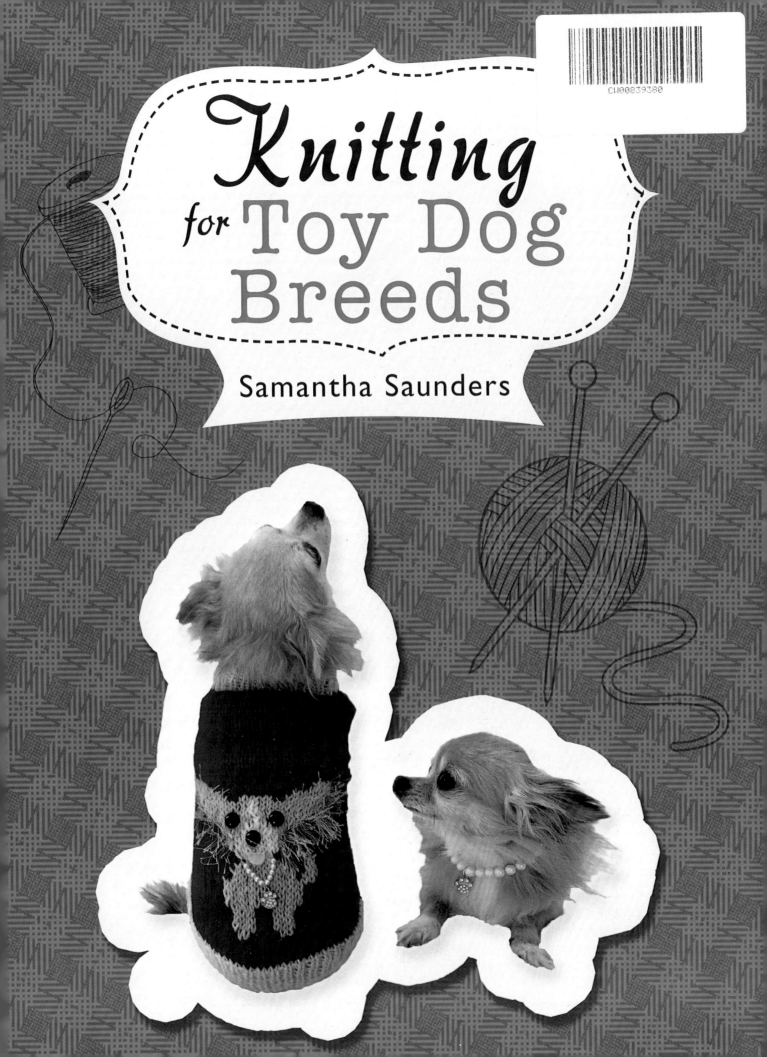

Knitting
for Toy Dog Breeds

Samantha Saunders

To order additional copies of this book, contact:
Xlibris
0800-056-3182
www.xlibrispublishing.co.uk
Orders@ Xlibrispublishing.co.uk

Dedication

To Mum, Dad, and Lin,

Thank you for all your support and laughter,

And my brother Jonathan, for all the encouragement

Jazzie 1997–2006

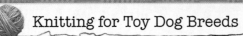

Introduction

Welcome to my pet knits. Whether you are a beginner or an expert knitter, these patterns are easily learnt and fun to do.

I got my first Chihuahua, Jazz, in 1997 and quickly realised that not only did she need clothes in winter, the limited ones on offer just would not fit or keep her warm enough.

When growing up, I remember my mum always had her knitting by her chair. I used to sit by her knee, watching in fascination as all sorts of her creations would grow: blankets, cardigans, and sweaters for my dad, my nephews, and I.

When finally I was ready, my mum had taught me to knit, and although I enjoyed it, I just couldn't keep the enthusiasm up, as a sweater for myself took me months to knit. But maybe a small sweater for my Chihuahua wouldn't be as time consuming. So with my newly purchased knitting needles, I began to design my first pet sweater. Not only would it keep her warm, but she would look stylish too!

My love for knitting and designing the patterns inserts and knits grew. I found I was knitting up a sweater in an evening; soon, she had more sweaters than me. They knitted up so fast; gone were the days of yarn sitting forlornly in the corner, abandoned from a sweater project that I had lost interest in. As my love for knitting grew, my patterns evolved as I tweaked and refined them, as at that point, I had four Chihuahuas, from one of ten pounds to one of three pounds. They all needed different types. I found that some didn't get on with a hoodie, and one couldn't wear sleeves, etc. When dressing any pet, the most important issue to me is that they are comfortable and happy; the sweaters must keep them warm and be functional and in no way impede their movement.

I also enjoy making pet toys, as I found all the store-bought ones seemed too big for my Chihuahuas' small mouths; they wouldn't play with any of their store-bought toys, especially balls.

The idea came to me when I left my then 8 month puppy, Am's, in the living room. I was gone for three minutes, and I heard a commotion. I rushed back to the living room, where I found my Chihuahua Am's looking especially pleased with herself. Yarn spilled across the room, she was splat out in the middle of it, with yarn on her head, in her mouth, over her back. She looked at me with big cheeky eyes, looking so pleased with herself. Jazz, being the older and wiser Chihuahua, sat on the couch looking disapprovingly at her and then at me, like 'It so wasn't me, Mum!' I noticed some yarn poking out from under her also!

So again, I got out my yarn and knitted them mice, bones, balls, and toys in all shapes and sizes. Needless to say, they were an instant hit with my Chihuahuas. They even enjoyed the misshapen ones as I refined the patterns. Yarn toys are still a big hit with all my Chihuahuas. Even my parents' Jack Russells Spot and Ben, and their cat Charlie enjoys playing with them!

I enjoy creating patterns and toys and wanted to share them and so decided to write a few down, which I present here to you, my reader.

So, grab a cuppa, some yarn and needles, and let's go . . .

Contents

Measuring Your Pet for the Perfect Fit

I have seen many methods for measuring pets, all good, but for me, I have found that the best way to measure (see diagram) is from the base of the neck to the base of the tail. When I make the sweaters, I always state this as the length size and never include the neck; this way, you shape the sweater better and add ribbing for different styles, e.g. a short neck or roll neck, etc.

The girth measurement I take from just behind the front legs, as this is the widest part of the dog, and of course the neck measurement. I always make the neck a little bigger than the actual measurement, as it needs to fit over the dog's head, and from experience with my apple-headed Chihuahuas, it's no fun trying on a sweater that is too small to fit over a squirming pet's head!

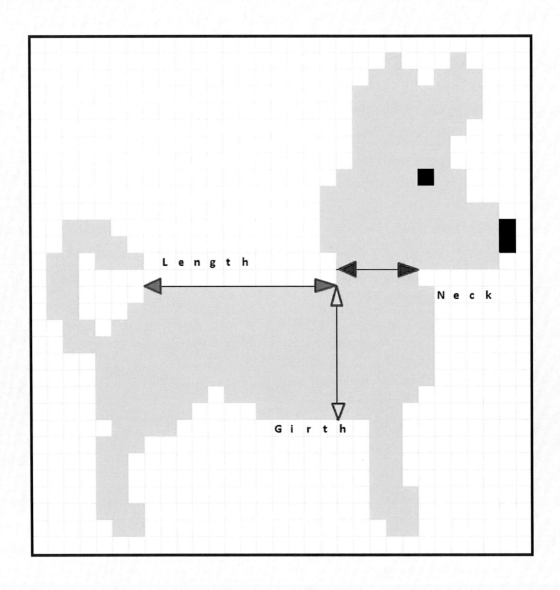

Sleeves

	4"	6"	7"	8"	9"	10"	12"	14"
Barely there c/o	24	26	26	28	28	32	34	36
Mini c/o	18	18	18	20	20	22	24	24
Short c/o	18	18	18	20	20	22	24	24
Medium c/o	18	18	18	20	20	22	24	24
Long c/o	18	18	18	20	20	20	22	22
Cone c/o	18	18	18	20	20 Add 2 rows	20 Add 4 rows	22 Add 4 rows	22 Add 4 rows
Ra Ra c/o	50	60	60	66	66 Add 2 rows	70 Add 2 rows	70 Add 2 rows	76 Add 2 rows

I find my dogs all have different requirements, especially when it comes to sleeves, so I have put together a section dedicated to different types of sleeves, so when knitting a sweater, you can choose the best sleeves to suit your pet. Just cast on (c/o) the amount from the table, and then choose any of the following:

Remember, with all sleeves, leave a small amount of yarn attached when binding on (b/o) for sewing together.

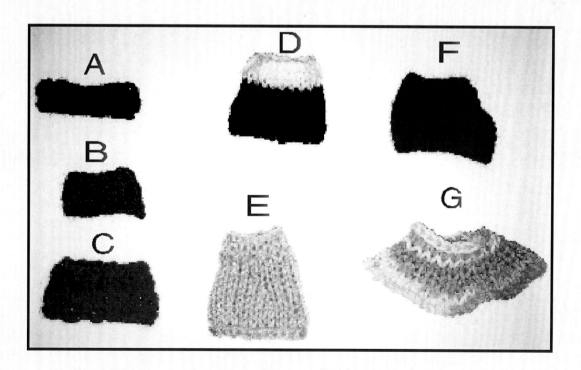

A	B	C	D
Barely There	Mini	Short	Medium
E	F	G	
Long	Cone	Rara	

Barely There

On 4 mm knitting needles, c/o your required number of stitches (sts).

Row 1   knit (k)

Row 2   k

B/o (bind off

Mini Sleeves

On 4-mm knitting needles, c/o your required number of sts.

Row 1   k

Row 2   purl (p)

Row 3   increase one stitch at beginning, *k3 increase one stitch, *r

Row 4   p

b/o

Short Sleeves

On 3¼ mm knitting needles, c/o your required number of sts.

Row 1   *k1, p1, *r

Row 2   *p1, k1, *r

Change to 4 mm knitting needles.

Row 3   k

Row 4   p

Row 5   *increase one stitch and k, k7, *r, k3

Row 6   p

b/o

Medium Sleeves

On 3¼ mm knitting needles, c/o your required number of sts.

Row 1   *k2, p2, *r

Row 2   *p2, k2, *r

Change to 4 mm knitting needles.

Row 3   k
Row 4   p
Row 5   k
Row 6   p
Row 7   in k, increase first and last stitch
Row 8   p
Row 9   in k, increase first and last stitch
Row 10   p
b/o

Long Sleeves

On 3¼ mm knitting needles, c/o your required number of sts.

Row 1   *k1, p1, *r

Repeat Row 1 for three more rows.

Row 5   k
Row 6   p
Row 7   *k6, m1 (make 1), *r
Row 8   p
Row 9   k6, m1, k8, m1, k6
Row 10   p
Row 11   k4, m1, k14, m1, k4
Row 12   p
b/o

Cone Sleeves

On 4-mm knitting needles, c/o sts.
Row 1   *k2, p2, *r
Row 2   *p2, k2, *r
Row 3   k
Row 4   p
Row 5   k4, m1 (and k it), k12, m1 (and k it), k4
Row 6   p
Row 7   k4, m1 (and k it), k12, m1 (and k it), k4

Row 8	p
Row 9	k4, m1 (and k it), k12, m1 (and k it), k4
Row 10	p
Row 11	k
Row 12	p
b/o	

Ra-ra Sleeves

On 4-mm knitting needles, c/o sts.

Row 1	k
Row 2	p
Row 3	*k2 tog (knit two together), *r
Row 4	*p2, p2 tog, *r
Row 5	k
Row 6	p
Row 7	k
Row 8	p
b/o	

Sewing the Sweater Together

All sweaters need to be sewn together basically the same way.

I start by tidying all yarn threads. The more colour yarns you use, the more threads there will be to tidy. The only yarn I keep long will be at the neck of the sweater, for sewing together.

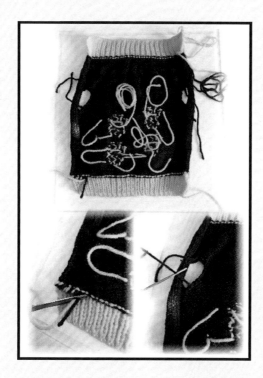

Working with the sweater inside out and starting at the neck, sew the sweater together, sewing in any loose one-inch threads into the seam (especially when working with multiple colour yarns).

The yarn at the base I thread into the seam, along the base ribbing. Leave the thread at the neck long, as we will be using this to sew up with. With a dual-colour sweater, where ribbing is different from the main body colour yarn, leave a long piece of yarn for sewing the main body of the sweater up with.

Leaving the yarn at the neck long to sew up with, if a dual colour, then leave enough of both colours for sewing up. Make sure the sweater is inside out. Work from the neck ribbing towards the base; when you reach the end, tie off and thread the yarn back through the seam, about 1½" then cut the yarn and the end disappears back into the seam for a clean finish.

When it comes to the sleeves, the best way to do this is when casting on leave a long tail of yarn; this can then be used to sew the sleeve together. Again, if you are using two colours, leave enough of both. With the sleeve inside out, start sewing together from the c/o row. When reaching the base, tie off, and with the seam facing the base of the sweater, attach the sleeve to the sweater. I usually hold the sleeve in place and, starting at the seam, work around clockwise. At the end, tie off, and as we did with the main sweater, sew back into the seam about an inch, cut the yarn, and again the tail of yarn disappears.

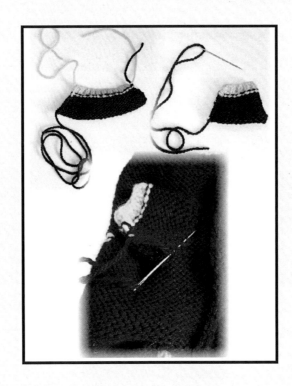

Pom-pom

Length 8″

The sweater photographed is eight inches in length.

Items you will need:

3¼ mm knitting needles
4 mm knitting needles
30 gm double knit yarn
Threading yarn needle
Sewing needle
Scissors
Pencil and paper

With 3¼ mm needles, cast on forty-four sts.
For the next six rows, work the waist ribbing.

Row 1   RS (right side) *k2, p2 *r
Row 2   WS (wrong side) *p2, k2 *r

Tip

Take the tail of yarn and work with double yarn into the pattern for four sts, then leave for trimming at the end of completed sweater. Continue working the pattern with your single yarn.

Continue knitting these two rows 1&2 for four more rows.

Now change to 4 mm needles and work in stocking stitch (stst).

Row 7   rs K
Row 8   ws P

Continue rows 7&8 for four more rows

Row 13   increase 5 sts at the start of your K row K to end   (53 sts)
Row 14   increase 5 sts at the start of your P row P to end   (58 sts)
Row 15   K
Row 16   P

Repeat rows 15&16 for eight more rows.

Shaping the Arm Holes (back)

Take the first 7 sts and place on a stitch holder; leave enough yarn attached to knit up later and cut, next cut approximately fifty-five inches of yarn to use later on the other arm hole.

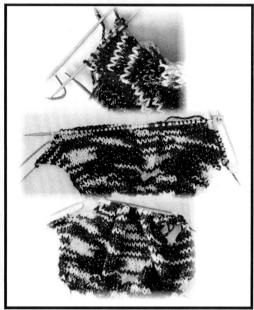

Row 25	k2t k40 k2t Place the remaining seven stitches on stitch holder.	
Row 26	p2t p38 p2t	
Row 27	k2t k36 k2t	
Row 28	p	
Row 29	k	
Row 30	in p m1 at beg (beginning) and end	(40 sts)
Row 31	in k m1 at beg and end	(42 sts)
Row 32	in p m1 at beg and end	(44 sts)

Cut yarn.

Shaping the Arm Holes (sides)

Take the sevem on the right side (rs) and put back on to the 4 mm knitting needle. With the yarn we left on these stitches, we begin shaping:

Row 25	k5 k2t (rs)	
Row 26	p2t p4 (wrong side (ws))	
Row 27	k3 k2t	
Row 28	p	
Row 29	k	
Row 30	p, m1 at beg	(5 sts)
Row 31	k, m1 at end	(6 sts)
Row 32	p m1 at beg	(7 sts)

Take the other seven on the stitch holder and put back on to the 4 mm knitting needle. With the yarn cut earlier, work these stitches. We begin shaping the second arm hole.

Row 25	k2t k5 (rs)
Row 26	p4 p2t (ws)
Row 27	k2t k3

Row 28	p	
Row 29	k	
Row 30	p m1 at end	(5 sts)
Row 31	k m1 at beg	(6 sts)
Row 32	p m1 at end	(7 sts)

Leaving the 7 sts we just worked on the knitting needle, pass back on the 44 and 7 sts we placed on the stitch holder.

Attach the main yarn and now we join all the three parts.

| Row 33 | rs k (as you knit across, tie off loose ends to working yarn) |
| Row 34 | ws p |

Continue in stst for another six rows.

Row 35	rs k1, *k5 k2t *r k1	(50 sts)
Row 36	ws p	
Row 37	k1, *k5 k2t *r	(42 sts)
Row 38	p	
Row 39	k	
Row 40	p	

Ribbing

Change to 3¼ mm knitting needles.

| Row 41 | *k2 p2 *r |
| Row 42 | *p2 k2 *r |

Repeat these two rows four more times.
B/o leave enough yarn to sew sweater up.

Short Sleeves

On 3¼ mm knitting needles, c/o 20 sts.

| Row 1 | *k1, p1, *r |
| Row 2 | *p1, k1, *r |

Change to 4 mm knitting needles.

Row 3	k
Row 4	p
Row 5	*Increase one stitch and k, k7, *r, k3
Row 6	p

b/o

Repeat these six rows for the second sleeve.

The Chihuahua

Length 12″

Items you will need:

3¼ mm knitting needles
4 mm knitting needles
60 gm double knit yarn
Yarn needle
Sewing needle
White cotton thread
Scissors
Pencil and paper
3 domed buttons
Shearing elastic
10 beads
Charm x 1

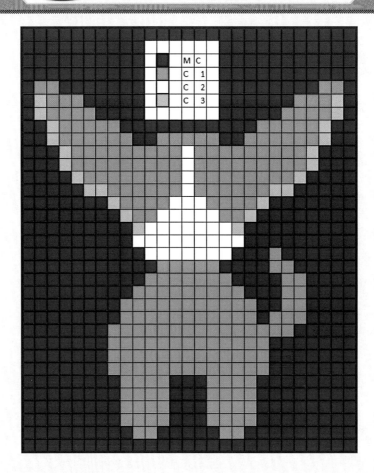

With 3¼ mm needles, cast on 51 sts.

For the next six rows, work the waist ribbing.

Row 1   rs *k1, p1 *r
Row 2   ws *p1, k1 *r

(Take the tail of yarn and work with double yarn into the pattern for 4 sts, then leave for trimming at the end of completed sweater. Continue working the pattern with your single yarn.)

Continue knitting these two rows until eight more rows are completed.

Now change to 4 mm needles and work in stst.

Row 11   rs k
Row 12   ws p

Repeat rows 11 and 12 four more times.

Chihuahua Pattern

Row 17   (rs)   k21 mc, k2 c1, k5 mc, k2 c1, k21 mc
Row 18   (ws)   p20 mc, p4 c1, p3 mc, p4 c1, p20 mc
Row 19   k20 mc, k4 c1, k3 mc, k4 c1, k20 mc

Row 20	p20 mc, p4 c1, p3 mc, p4 c1, p20 mc
Row 21	k20 mc, k4 c1, k3 mc, k4 c1, k20 mc
Row 22	p19 mc, p13 c1, p19 mc
Row 23	k19 mc, k13 c1, k19 mc
Row 24	p19 mc, p13 c1, p19 mc
Row 25	k17 mc, k15 c1, k19 mc
Row 26	p20 mc, p11 c1, p1 mc, p3 c1, p16 mc
Row 27	m5 (make 5) sts including these sts, k21 mc, k2 c1, k2 mc, k11 c1, k20 mc
Row 28	m5 sts including these sts, p26 mc, p9 c1, p3 mc, p2 c1, p21 mc
Row 29	k21 mc, k2 c1, k4 mc, k7 c1, k27 mc
Row 30	p28 mc, p5 c1, p4 mc, p2 c1, p22 mc
Row 31	k23 mc, k1 c1, k3 mc, k7 c2, k27 mc
Row 32	p26 mc, p9 c2, p26 mc
Row 33	k26 mc, k1 c3, k7 c2, k1 c3, k26 mc
Row 34	p25 mc, p1 c3, p2 c1, p5 c2, p2 c1, p1 c3, p25 mc
Row 35	k24 mc, k1 c3, k4 c1, k3 c2, k4 c1, k1 c3, k24 mc
Row 36	p22 mc, p2 c3, p6 c1, p1 c2, p6 c1, p2 c3, p22
Row 37	k21 mc, k1 c3, k8 c1, k1 c2, k8 c1, k1 c3, k21 mc
Row 38	p20 mc, p1 c3, p9 c1, p1 c2, p9 c1, p1 c3, p20 mc
Row 39	k20 mc, k1 c3, k9 c1, k1 c2, k9 c1, k1 c3, k20 mc
Row 40	p19 mc, p1 c3, p6 c1, p2 mc, p5 c1, p2 mc, p6 c1, p1 c3, p19 mc
Row 41	k19 mc, k1 c3, k5 c1, k11 mc, k5 c1, k1 c3, k19 mc
Row 42	p18 mc, p1 c3, p4 c1, p15 mc, p4 c1, p1 c3, p18 mc
Row 43	k18 mc, k1 c3, k3 c1, k17 mc, k3 c1, k1 c3, k18 mc
Row 44	p18 mc, p2 c1, p21 mc, p2 c1, p18 mc

Shaping for Front Leg Holes

We now need to shape the arm holes; we do this by placing the first 9 sts on to a stitch holder and winding enough yarn off the main ball before cutting and leaving. Wind enough yarn for working the other side and cut; leave this to one side for use later.

Attach the main ball of yarn to the remaining 52 sts.

Row 45	k2 tog k39 k2 tog	Hold last 9 sts on stitch holder for working later.
Row 46	p2 tog p37 p2 tog	
Row 47	k2 tog k35 k2 tog	
Row 48	p	
Row 49	k	
Row 50	p	

Row 51	in k m1 at beg and end	(39 sts)
Row 52	in p m1 at beg and end	(41 sts)
Row 53	in k m1 at beg and end	(43 sts)

Hold this work on needle and work first on the rs 9 sts on our stitch holder. Place these 9 sts on to a 4 mm knitting needle. Work rows as follows:

Row 45	k7, k2 tog	
Row 46	p2 tog, p6	
Row 47	k5, k2 tog	
Row 48	p	
Row 49	k	
Row 50	p	
Row 51	m1 at end in k	(7 sts)
Row 52	m1 at beg in p	(8 sts)
Row 53	m1 at end in k	(9 sts)

Place back on to stitch holder.

Now we will work the other 9 sts, working rs.

Row 45	k2 tog, k7	
Row 46	p6, p2 tog	
Row 47	k2 tog, k5	
Row 48	p	
Row 49	k	
Row 50	p	
Row 51	m1 at beg in k	(7 sts)
Row 52	m1 at end in p	(8 sts)
Row 53	m1 at beg in k	(9 sts)

Now we join all three parts together, totalling 61 sts.

Row 54	p61 sts, tying the loose threads each end as you work across to main yarn
Row 55	k
Row 56	p

Repeat rows 53 and 54 for another twelve rows.

Row 69	k1, *k9 k2 tog *r, k2
Row 70	p
Row 71	*k7 k2 tog *r
Row 72	p in white yarn

Change to 3¼ mm knitting needles.

Ribbing

*k1, p1, *r
*k1, p1, *r

Repeat these two rows for the next eight rows.

B/o cut yarn, leaving enough to sew up later.

Short Sleeves

C/o 24 sts in MC

Row 1	k1, p1
Row 2	r Row 1
Row 3	k
Row 4	p
Row 5	in k *increase 1 stitch (st) k8, *r (27 sts)
Row 6	p

B/o cut yarn, leaving enough to sew up later

Repeat these six rows for the second sleeve.

Ra-ra Dress

The sweater photographed is eight inches in length.

Items you will need:

4 mm knitting needles
80 gm double knit yarn
Threading yarn needle
Sewing needle
Scissors
Sequins
Felt
Beads
Pins
Pencil and paper

With 4 mm needles, cast on 136 sts.

Row 1   RS k
Row 2   WS p

Repeat rows 1 and 2 four more times.

Row 7   *k2 tog x5, sl, k2 tog psso (pass slip stitch over), *r, k2 tog x3   (63 sts)

Row 8   *p7, p2 tog, *r   (56 sts)

Row 9   k

Row 10   p

Repeat rows 9 and 10 eighteen more times.

Shaping the Front Leg Holes (Back)

Take the first and last 9 sts and place on a stitch holder. Leave enough yarn attached to knit up later and cut; then cut approximately fifty-five inches of yarn to use later on the other arm hole.

Row 29   k2 tog, k35, k2 tog

Row 30   p2 tog, p33, p2 tog

Row 31   k2 tog, k31, k2 tog

Row 32   p2 tog, p29, p2 tog

Row 33   k

Row 34   p

Row 35   k

Row 36   in p m1 at beg and end

Row 37   in k m1 at beg and end

Row 38   in p m1 at beg and end

Row 39   in k m1 at beg and end k

Shaping the Front Leg Holes (Sides)

Take the first 9 sts from the stitch holder and put back on to the 4 mm knitting needle. With the yarn we left on these stitches, we begin shaping.

Row 29   k7, k2 tog (rs)

Row 30   p2 tog, p6 (ws)

Row 31   k5, k2 tog

Row 32   p2 tog, p4

Row 33   k

Row 34   p

Row 35   k

Row 36   p m1 at beg

Row 37   k m1 at end

Row 38   p m1 at beg

Row 39   k m1 at end

Take the other nine on the stitch holder and put back on to the 4 mm knitting needle. With the yarn we cut earlier, we work these stitches. We begin shaping the second leg hole.

Row 29	k2 tog, k7 (rs)
Row 30	p6, p2 tog (ws)
Row 31	k2 tog, k5
Row 32	p4, p2 tog
Row 33	k
Row 34	p
Row 35	k
Row 36	p m1 at end
Row 37	k m1 at beg
Row 38	p m1 at end
Row 39	k m1 at beg

Join all the three parts.

Row 40	rs p (as you knit across, tie off loose ends to working yarn)
Row 41	ws k
Row 42	p

Repeat rows 41 and 42 for six rows.

Row 49	k1, *k5, k2t, *r
Row 50	p
Row 51	*k5, k2t, *r
Row 52	p

Ribbing

Change to 3¼ mm knitting needles and c1.

Row 53	*k2, p2, *r
Row 54	*p2, k2, *r

Repeat these two rows six more times.

B/o leaving enough yarn to sew sweater up.

Making the Ruffles

C/o 116 sts.

Row 1   k
Row 2   p

Repeat these two rows four more times.

B/o, leaving enough yarn to attach the ruffles later.

Ra-ra Sleeves

On 4 mm knitting needles, c/o 66 sts.

Row 1   k
Row 2   p
Row 3   *k2 tog, *r
Row 4   *p2, p2 tog, *r
Row 5   k
Row 6   p
Row 7   k
Row 8   p

b/o.

Sewing this sweater together is slightly different from the others, as it has more parts to it.

After tidying loose yarn threads, we start sewing the ruffles on to the skirt. I find laying the dress flat and pinning the ruffles on to the sweater is the simplest way, evenly distributing it, to give that gathered look. Once you have the first ruffle in place, put the second above it, and again pin and sew it on.

Next, we sew the sweater from the neck, and working down, make sure to catch the ruffles together and sew them also.

Sew the sleeves on and then sew the appliqué of your choice on.

Making the Crown Appliqué

You will need:

Felt
Sequins
A felt tip pen
Scissors
Cotton thread and needle
Pins

Draw out your crown shape on paper; attach this template to your felt.

Draw around your template with a felt tip pen. When happy, remove your template and cut out your shape. This side may have some felt tip pen marks left, so we will turn it over and use the other side.

Taking your sequins, sew them on to your crown, overlapping them slightly until you have your shape covered. If any protrudes over your felt, simply trim to maintain your original shape.

Attach to dress.

The Love Bug

Length 10″

The sweater photographed is ten inches in length.

Items you will need:

3¼ mm knitting needles

4 mm knitting needles

40 gm double knit yarn, three colours

Threading yarn needle

Sewing needle

Googly eyes

Scissors

Pencil and paper

C/o 48 sts on 3¼ mm knitting needles.

Ribbing   in C1

Row 1   RS *k2, p2, *r

Repeat Row 1 for seven more rows.

Change to 4 mm knitting needles, mc.
The main sweater is knitted in stst.

Row 9   k
Row 10   p

Repeat these two rows for the next four rows.

Starting the Love Bug

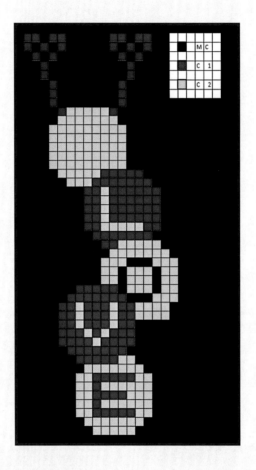

Row 15   (rs) k20 mc, k5c2, k23 mc
Row 16   (ws) p22 mc, p7c2, p19 mc
Row 17   k18 mc, k2c2, k5c1, k2c2, k21 mc
Row 18   p21 mc, p2c2, p1c1, p6c2, p18 mc
Row 19   k18 mc, k3c2, k4c1, k2c2, k21 mc
Row 20   p21 mc, p2c2, p1c1, p6c2, p18 mc
Row 21   k18 mc, k2c2, k5c1, k2c2, k21 mc
Row 22   p22 mc, p7c2, p19 mc
Row 23   k20 mc, k2c2, k5c1, k21 mc
Row 24   p20 mc, p7c1, p21 mc
Row 25   k20 mc, k4c1, k1c2, k4c1, k19 mc
Row 26   p19 mc, p3c1, p1c2, p1c1, p1c2, p3c1, p20 mc

Row 27	k20 mc, k2c1, k1c2, k3c1, k1c2, k2c1, k19 mc
Row 28	p19 mc, p2c1, p1c2, p3c1, p1c2, p2c1, p4c2, p16 mc
Row 29	(rs) m5 sts at beginning, including these work patterns as follows: k21 mc, k4c2, k2c1, k1c2, k3c1, k1c2, k2c1, k19 mc
Row 30	(ws) m5 sts at beginning, including these work patterns as follows: p25 mc, p7c1, p3 mc, p3c2, p20 mc
Row 31	k20 mc, k2c2, k1 mc, k3c2, k1 mc, k5c1, k26 mc
Row 32	p29 mc, p2c2, p1 mc, p3c2, p1 mc, p2c2, p20 mc
Row 33	k20 mc, k2c2, k1 mc, k3c2, k1 mc, k2c2, k29 mc
Row 34	p29 mc, p3c2, p3 mc, p3c2, p20 mc
Row 35	k21 mc, k7c2, k30 mc
Row 36	p29 mc, p2c1, p5c2, p22 mc

Shaping for Front Leg Holes

Hold the first and last 9 sts on two stitch holders, leaving the remaining 40 sts on your main knitting needle to be worked as follows:

Row 37	k2 togmc, k12 mc, k7c1, k17 mc, k2 togmc	(38 sts)
Row 38	p2 togmc, p15 mc, p2c1, p5c2, p2c1, p10 mc, p2 togmc	(36 sts)
Row 39	k2 togmc, k9 mc, k6c1, k1c2, k2c1, k14 mc, k2 togmc	(34 sts)
Row 40	p2 togmc, p13 mc, p2c1, p1c2, p6c1, p8 mc, p2 togmc	(32 sts)
Row 41	k9 mc, k6c1, k1c2, k2c1, k14 mc	
Row 42	p14 mc, p2c1, p1c2, p6c1, p9 mc	
Row 43	k10 mc, k7c1, k3c2, k12 mc	
Row 44	p13 mc, p5c2, p5c1, p9 mc	
Row 45	m1 at beg and end, including these stitches, work as follows: k16 mc, k9c2, k9 mc	(34 sts)
Row 46	m1 at beg and end, including these stitches, work as follows: p10 mc, p9c2, p17 mc	(36 sts)
Row 47	m1 at beg and end, including these stitches, work as follows: k18 mc, k9c2, k11 mc	(38 sts)
Row 48	m1 at beg and end, including these stitches, work as follows: p12 mc, p9c2, p19 mc	(40 sts)

Shape first 9 sts (rs).

Place the first 9 sts on to a 4 mm knitting needle and work in (mc) as follows:

Row 37	k7, k2 tog
Row 38	p2 tog, p6
Row 39	k5, k2 tog

Row 40	p2 tog, p4	
Row 41	k	
Row 42	p	
Row 43	k	
Row 44	p	
Row 45	k m1 at end	(6 sts)
Row 46	p m1 at beg	(7 sts)
Row 47	k m1 at end	(8 sts)
Row 48	p m1 at beg	(9 sts)

Shape the last 9 sts (rs).

Place the last 9 sts on to a 4 mm knitting needle and work in (mc) as follows:

Row 37	k2 tog, k7	
Row 38	p6, p2 tog	
Row 39	k2 tog, k5	
Row 40	p4, p2 tog	
Row 41	k	
Row 42	p	
Row 43	k	
Row 44	p	
Row 45	k m1 at beg	(6 sts)
Row 46	p m1 at end	(7 sts)
Row 47	k m1 at beg	(8 sts)
Row 48	p m1 at end	(9 sts)

Now on Row 49, we will join all three parts, totalling 58 sts.

Row 49	k26 mc, k9c2, k23 mc
Row 50	p24 mc, p7c2, p27 mc
Row 51	k24 mc, k1c1, k5c2, k1c1, k27 mc
Row 52	p23 mc, p1c1, p7 mc, p1c1, p26 mc
Row 53	k26 mc, k1c1, k7 mc, k1c1, k23 mc
Row 54	p23 mc, p1c1, p7 mc, p1c1, p26 mc
Row 55	k25 mc, k1c1, k9 mc, k1c1, k22 mc
Row 56	p22 mc, p1c1, p9 mc, p1c1, p25 mc
Row 57	k24 mc, k1c1, k1 mc, k1c1, k7 mc, k1c1, k1 mc, k1c1, k21 mc
Row 58	p20 mc, p1c1, p1 mc, p1c1, p1 mc, p1c1, p5 mc, p1c1, p1 mc, p1c1, p1 mc, p1c1, p23 mc
Row 59	k23 mc, k2c1, k1 mc, k2c1, k5 mc, k2c1, k1 mc, k2c1, k20 mc

Row 60	*k5, k2 tog, *r, k2	(50 sts)
Row 61	p	
Row 62	*k5, k2 tog, *r, k1	(43 sts)

Cut black yarn, leaving enough to sew sweater up. Now change to C1 yarn.

| Row 63 | p |

Ribbing

Change to 3¼ mm knitting needles.

Row 1	k2 tog, k1, p2, *k2, p2, *r
Row 2	*p2, k2, *r
Row 3	*k2, p2, *r

Repeat Row 2&3 for 5 more rows.

B/o cut yarn, leaving enough to sew up the sweater neck in red.

Medium Sleeves

On 3¼ mm, c/o 22.

Row 1	*k2, p2, *r
Row 2	*p2, k2, *r
Row 3	*k2, p2, *r
Row 4	*p2, k2, *r
Row 5	k
Row 6	p
Row 7	in k increase first and last st
Row 8	p
Row 9	in k increase first and last st
Row 10	p

| B/o | leave a tail of yarn for sewing up the sleeves later. |

Repeat for a second sleeve.

Snowman

This makes a 9″ sweater.

Items you will need:

3¼ mm knitting needles

4 mm knitting needles

30 gm double knit yarn, three colours

Threading yarn needle

Sewing needle

Cotton thread

Pom poms 3x green 1x orange

Googly eyes

Scissors

Pencil and paper

C/o 45 sts on 3¼ mm knitting needles mc.

Ribbing

Row 1   *k1, p1, *r

Repeat Row 1 for five more rows

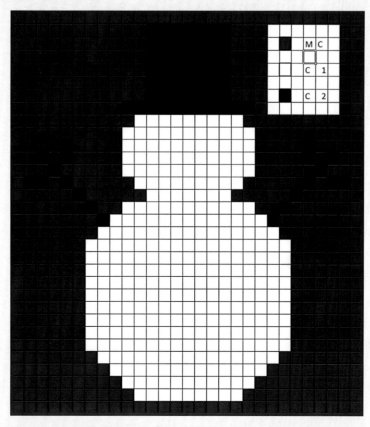

Change to 4 mm knitting needles.

Row 7	k18 mc, k9c1, k18 mc
Row 8	p17 mc, p11c1, p17 mc
Row 9	k16 mc, k13c1, k16 mc
Row 10	p15 mc, p15c1, p15 mc
Row 11	k14 mc, k17c1, k14 mc
Row 12	p14 mc, p17c1, p14 mc
Row 13	k14 mc, k17c1, k14 mc
Row 14	p14 mc, p17c1, p14 mc
	m6 sts at beg, including these k as follows:
Row 15	k20 mc, k17c1, k14 mc
	m6 sts at beg, including these p as follows:
Row 16	p20 mc, p17c1, p20 mc
Row 17	k20 mc, k17c1, k20 mc
Row 18	p20 mc, p17c1, p20 mc
Row 19	k20 mc, k17c1, k20 mc
Row 20	p21 mc, p15c1, p21 mc
Row 21	k21 mc, k1c2, k13c1, k1c2, k21 mc
Row 22	p20 mc, p1c2, p2 mc, p11c1, p2 mc, p1c2, p20 mc
Row 23	k19 mc, k1c2, k5 mc, k7c1, k5 mc, k1c2, k19 mc
Row 24	p15 mc, p2c2, p1 mc, p1c2, p5 mc, p9c1, p5 mc, p1c2, p1 mc, p2c2, p15 mc
Row 25	k17 mc, k1c2, k5 mc, k11c1, k5 mc, k1c2, k17 mc
Row 26	p16 mc, p1c2, p1 mc, p1c2, p4 mc, p11c1, p4 mc, p1c2, p1 mc, p1c2, p16 mc
Row 27	k18 mc, k1c2, k4 mc, k11c1, k4 mc, k1c2, k18 mc
Row 28	p23 mc, p11c1, p23 mc
Row 29	k24 mc, k9c1, k24 mc
Row 30	p23 mc, p11c2, p23 mc
Row 31	k25 mc, k7c2, k25 mc
Row 32	p25 mc, p7c2, p25 mc

Shaping for Front Leg Holes

Hold the first and last 7 sts on two stitch holders, leaving the remaining 43 sts on your main knitting needle to be worked as follows:

Row 33	k2 togmc, k16 mc, k7c2, k16 mc, k2 togmc
Row 34	p2 togmc, p15 mc, p7c2, p15 mc, p2 togmc
Row 35	k2 togmc, k14 mc, k7c2, k14 mc, k2 togmc
Row 36	p15 mc, p7c2, p15 mc
Row 37	k
Row 38	p
Row 39	k

Row 40	m1 at beg and end p	(39 sts
Row 41	m1 at beg and end k	(41 sts)
Row 42	m1 at beg and end p	(43 sts)

Place the first 7 sts on to a 4 mm knitting needle and work in (mc) as follow:

Row 33	k5, k2 tog	
Row 34	p2 tog, p4	
Row 35	k3, k2 tog	
Row 36	p	
Row 37	k	
Row 38	p	
Row 39	k	
Row 40	p m1 at beg	(5 sts)
Row 41	k m1 at end	(6 sts)
Row 42	p m1 at beg	(7 sts)

Place the last 7 sts on to a 4 mm knitting needle and work in (mc) as follows:

Row 33	k2 tog, k5	
Row 34	p4, p2 tog	
Row 35	k2 tog, k3	
Row 36	p	
Row 37	k	
Row 38	P	
Row 39	k	
Row 40	p m1 at end	(5 sts)
Row 41	k m1 at beg	(6 sts)
Row 42	p m1 at end	(7 sts)

Join all three parts.

| Row 43 | k |
| Row 44 | p |

Repeat rows 43 and 44 ten more times.

Row 55	*k5, k2 tog, *r, k1
Row 56	p
Row 57	*k5, k2 tog, *r
Row 58	p

Ribbing

Change to 3¼ mm knitting needles.

Row 1   *k1, p1, *r

Repeat Row 1 for five more rows.

b/o cut yarn, leaving enough to sew up the sweater.

Medium Sleeves

On 3¼ mm, c/o 22.

Row 1   *k1, p1, *r

Repeat Row 1 for three more rows.

Row 5   k
Row 6   p
Row 7   in k, increase first and last st
Row 8   p
Row 9   in k, increase first and last st
Row 10   p

b/o   leaving a tail of yarn for sewing up later.

Repeat for second sleeve.

Snowman Accessories

Place on the googly eyes; sew three green pom poms on-to the body, and an orange pom pom for the carrot nose. To make the scarf, cut six 7" pieces of yarn. I have chosen red, white, and green. We will be using all three strands each side. Thread each one through the sweater one at a time, where you wish your scarf to be, bringing both ends out. Make them equal, and when you have all three colours doubled through, tie them in place, then grouping the two red, two white, and two green together, plait them. When you have a long enough scarf, tie off the ends, trim to neaten, then fray the yarn ends. Repeat this for the other side, and when done, tie scarf in place. See picture.

Knitted Toy Mouse

Items you will need:

4 mm knitting needles
15 gm double knit yarn
Threading yarn needle
Sewing needle
Scissors
Toy filling
Pencil and paper

C/o 10 sts.

Row 1	k	
Row 2	*k2, increase 1 st, *r	(14 sts)
Row 3	k	
	R Row 3 two more times.	
Row 6	*k2, increase 1 st, *r	(20 sts)
Row 7	k	
	R Row 7 two more times.	
Row 10	*k3 increase 1 st *r, k2	(26 sts)
Row 11	k	
	R Row 11 five more times.	
Row 17	*k2 k2 tog k3 k2 tog *r, k1	
Row 18	k	
	R Row 18 six more times.	
Row 25	k decrease first and last stitch	
Row 26	k decrease first and last stitch	
Row 27	* k1 k2 tog *r, k1	(12 sts)
Row 28	k	
	R Row 28 two more times.	

Row 31   *k1 k2 tog *r   (8)
Row 32   k
            R Row 32 one more time.
Row 34   k decrease first and last stitch
Row 35   k2 tog, k2, k2 tog
Row 36   k, k2 tog, k2 tog

B/o   Leave enough yarn to sew together.

Knitted Ears

C/o 5 sts.

Row 1   k
Row 2   k
Row 3   in k, increase first and last st
Row 4   k
            Repeat Row 4 four more times.

B/o   Leave enough yarn to sew with.

Repeat for second ear.

Assembling the Mouse

Start by sewing the mouse body inside out from the nose end. This is where we left the yarn for sewing together. When you have about an inch left, stop sewing; turn it the right way out and stuff with toy filling. When you have your mouse nice and full, sew the remaining inch up and knot, then thread the yarn through the mouse and cut. The yarn should slip back into the mouse, leaving no unsightly ends.

Next, take a knitted ear with the yarn on the curve of the ear. Thread it through to the base and cut.

Now take the yarn on the straight part of the ear. We will use this yarn to attach the ear to the body. Firstly, put the two corners of the base of the ear together and sew from the front to the back. Next, take the ear and attach it to the mouse body, fasten, thread the needle through the mouse, cut, and again the yarn should slip back into the mouse, leaving no unsightly ends.

Repeat for the second ear.

Eyes, Nose, Tail, and Whiskers

Taking a long piece of black yarn, sew three or four times into the nose area to create a nose, and without cutting the thread, feed the yarn needle inside the mouse to the eye area for the eyes. Again, without cutting the yarn, take the yarn and needle through the inside of the mouse all the way to the base of the mouse, bringing it out where you would like the tail to be. Sew three times, fasten off, and cut yarn to the desired length.

With another piece of black yarn about six inches, thread into the side of the nose area (see picture) where you would like the whiskers, having the yarn ends both go through the mouse on one side so they are equal length. Take the yarn needle out, tie together; then taking the yarn needle, fray the whiskers. Cut to desired length. My mouse whiskers are approximately 1½ in.

Repeat for the other side.

Cheeky Monkey

The sweater photographed is fourteen inches in length.

Items you will need:

3¼ mm knitting needles
4 mm knitting needles
55 gm chunky yarn, three colours
Threading yarn needle
Sewing needle
Googly eyes
Brown domed button
Scissors
Pencil and paper

C/o 63 sts on 3¼ mm knitting needles.

Ribbing

Green yarn (mc)

Row 1   *k1, p1, *r
Row 2   *p1, k1, *r

Repeat rows 1 and 2 for eight more rows.

Change to 4 mm knitting needles. The main sweater is knitted in stst.

Row 1   k(rs)
Row 2   p (ws)

Repeat these two rows for the next six rows.

Starting the pattern *(Row 9–16 monkey)*

Row 9   k25 mc, k1c1, k2 mc, k1c1, k1 mc, k1c1, k2 mc, k1c1, k25 mc

Row 10   p21 mc, p2c1, p2 mc, p1c1, p2 mc, p1c1, p1 mc, p1c1, p1 mc, p1c1, p2 mc, p4c1, p20 mc

Row 11   k16 mc, k1c1, k6 mc, k1c1, k3 mc, k2c1, k1 mc, k2c1, k1 mc, k1c1, k1 mc, k1c1, k2 mc, k1c1, k1 mc, k1c1, k3 mc, k1c1, k14 mc

Row 12   p14 mc, p1c1, p3 mc, p1c1, p1 mc, p1c1, p2 mc, p1c1, p1 mc, p2c1, p1 mc, p1c1, p1 mc, p1c1, p1 mc, p1c1, p2 mc, p3c1, p4 mc, p1c1, p16 mc

Row 13   k16 mc, k1c1, k6 mc, k1c1, k1 mc, k1c1, k2 mc, k1c1, k1 mc, k1c1, k2 mc, k1c1, k1 mc, k1c1, k2 mc, k1c1, k1 mc, k1c1, k1 mc, k1c1, k1 mc, k1c1, k14 mc

Row 14   p14 mc, p2c1, p1 mc, p2c1, p2 mc, p2c1, p12 mc, p4c1, p2 mc, p1c1, p1 mc, p1c1, p15 mc

At beg m6 sts, including these, work as follows:

Row 15   k20 mc, k1c1, k3 mc, k1c1, k21 mc, k1c1, k3 mc, k1c1, k14 mc

At beg m6 sts, including these, work as follows:

Row 16   p   (total 73 sts)

(Row 17–36 monkey's face)

Row 17   k34 mc, k5c1, k34 mc
Row 18   p33 mc, p7c1, p33 mc
Row 19   k32 mc, k1c1, k7c2, k1c1, k32 mc
Row 20   p31 mc, p1c1, p9c2, p1c1, p31 mc
Row 21   k30 mc, k1c1, k11c2, k1c1 k30 mc
Row 22   p29 mc, p1c1, p13c2, p1c1, p29 mc
Row 23   k29 mc, k1c1, k1c2, k1c1, k29 mc
Row 24   p29 mc, p1c1, p13c2, p1c1, p29 mc
Row 25   k30 mc, k1c1, k11c2, k1c1, k30 mc
Row 26   p31 mc, p2c1, p7c2, p2c1, p31 mc
Row 27   k30 mc, k3c1, k7c2, k3c1, k30 mc
Row 28   p27 mc, p5c1, p1c2, p1c1, p5c2, p1c1, p1c2, p5c1, p27 mc
Row 29   k26 mc, k6c1, k1c2, k2c1, k1c2, k1c1, k1c2, k2c1, k1c2, k6c1, k26 mc
Row 30   p26 mc, p2c1, p2c2, p2c1, p4c2, p1c1, p4c2, p2c1, p2c2, p2c1, p26 mc
Row 31   k26 mc, k2c1, k2c2, k3c1, k2c2, k3c1, k2c2, k3c1, k2c2, k2c1, k26 mc
Row 32   p26 mc, p21c1, p26 mc
Row 33   k27 mc, k3c1, k1 mc, k11c1, k1 mc, k3c1, k27 mc
Row 34   p32 mc, p9c1, p32 mc
Row 35   k33 mc, k7c1, k33 mc
Row 36   p34 mc, p5c1, p34 mc

Shaping for Front Leg Holes

Hold the first and last 9 sts on two stitch holders, leaving the remaining 55 sts on your main knitting needle to be worked as follows:

Row 37   k2 tog, k51, k2 tog
Row 38   p2 tog, p49, p2 tog
Row 39   k2 tog mc, k11 mc, k1c1, k23 mc, k3c1, k9 mc, k2 tog mc
Row 40   p9 mc, p1c1, p4 mc, p1c1, p2 mc, p1c1, p11 mc, p1c1, p2 mc, p1c1, p3 mc, p1c1, p12 mc
Row 41   k12 mc, k1c1, k4 mc, k1c1, k1 mc, k1c1, k1 mc, k4c1, k1 mc, k4c1, k1 mc, k1c1, k2 mc, k1c1, k4 mc, k1c1, k9 mc
Row 42   p9 mc, p1c1, p4 mc, p4c1, p1 mc, p1c1, p4 mc, p1c1, p4 mc, p2c1, p4 mc, p1c1, p1 mc, p1c1, p11 mc
Row 43   k10 mc, k1c1, k3 mc, k1c1, k2 mc, k1c1, k1 mc, k1c1, k2 mc,k3c1, k2 mc, k3c1, k1 mc, k1c1, k2 mc, k1c1, k1 mc, k3c1, k10 mc
Row 44   p14 mc, p1c1, p2 mc, p1c1, p1 mc, p1c1, p4 mc, p1c1, p4 mc, p1c1, p2 mc, p1c1, p16 mc

m1 at beg and end, including these, work as follows:

Row 45   k22 mc, k4c1, k1 mc, k4c1, k20 mc

m1 at beg and end, including these, work as follows:

Row 46   p   (53 sts)

m1 at beg and end, including these, work as follows:

Row 47   k   (55 sts)

Shape first 9 sts (rs).

Place the first 9 sts on to a 4 mm knitting needle and work in (mc) as follows:

Row 37	k7, k2t	
Row 38	p2 tog, p6	
Row 39	k5, k2 tog	
Row 40	p	
Row 41	k	
Row 42	p	
Row 43	k	
Row 44	p	
Row 45	K m1 at end	(7 sts)
Row 46	P m1 at beg	(8 sts)
Row 47	K m1 at end	(9 sts)

Shape last 9 sts (rs).

Place the last 9 sts on to a 4 mm knitting needle and work in (mc) as follows:

Row 37	k2 tog, k7	
Row 38	p6, p2 tog	
Row 39	k2 tog, k5	
Row 40	p	
Row 41	k	
Row 42	p	
Row 43	k	
Row 44	p	
Row 45	K m1 at beg	(7 sts)
Row 46	P m1 at end	(8 sts)
Row 47	K m1 at beg	(9 sts)
Row 48	p, joining all three parts	(73 sts)
Row 49	k	
Row 50	p	

Repeat rows 49 and 50 for sixteen more rows.

Row 67	k1, *k9, k2 tog, *r, k3
Row 68	p
Row 69	*k7, k2 tog, *r, k1
Row 70	p

Change to 3¼ mm knitting needles.

Ribbing

| Row 1 | *k1, p1, *r |
| Row 2 | *p1, k1 *r |

Repeat rows 1 and 2 for 9 more rows

b/o in p.

Long Sleeves

C/o 20 st on 4 mm knitting needles.

Ribbing

| Row 1 | *k1, p1, *r |

Repeat Row 1 for three more rows.

Row 5	k	
Row 6	p	
Row 7	k	
Row 8	p	
Row 9	k	
Row 10	p	
Row 11	in k m1 at beg and end	(22 sts)
Row 12	in p m1 at beg and end	(24 sts)
Row 13	in k m1 at beg and end	(26 sts)
Row 14	in p m1 at beg and end	(28 sts)

| B/o | Repeat for second sleeve. |

Now tidy and sew the sweater together. See page 11.

Snowflake (Girl-only Style)

This sweater will be six inches in length.

Items you will need:

3¼ mm knitting needles

4 mm knitting needles

20 gm double knit yarn, two colours

Threading yarn needle

Scissors

Pencil and paper

C/o 49 sts 4 mm knitting needles.

Starting   in Lilac Yarn (c1)

Row 1   rs k

Row 2   ws p

Row 3   k

Row 4   p

Row 5   *k2 tog, yfwd, k1, *r

Row 6   p

Row 7   k

Row 8   p

Row 9   Change to mc and k.
Row 10   p

Now we start the snowflake pattern.

Row 11   k23 mc, k1c1, k1 mc, k1c1, k23 mc
Row 12   p21 mc, p1c1, p1 mc, p1c1, p1 mc, p1c1, p1 mc, p1c1, p21 mc
Row 13   k18 mc, k1c1, k3 mc, k1c1, k1 mc, k1c1, k1 mc, k1c1, k3 mc, k1c1, k18 mc
Row 14   p19 mc, p1c1, p3 mc, p3c1, p3 mc, p1c1, p19 mc
Row 15   k20 mc, k1c1, k3 mc, k1c1, k3 mc, k1c1, k20 mc
Row 16   p17 mc, p1c1, p3 mc, p1c1, p2 mc, p1c1, p2 mc, p1c1, p3 mc, p1c1, p17 mc
Row 17   k18 mc, k1c1, k3 mc, k1c1, k1 mc, k1c1, k1 mc, k1c1, k3 mc, k1c1, k18 mc
Row 18   p16 mc, p2c1, p1 mc, p1c1, p4 mc, p1c1, p4 mc, p1c1, p1 mc, p2c1, p16 mc
Row 19   k18 mc, k6c1, k1 mc, k6c1, k18 mc
Row 20   p16 mc, p2c1, p1 mc, p1c1, p4 mc, p1c1, p4 mc, p1c1, p1 mc, p2c1, p16 mc

Shape for Front Leg Holes

Hold the first and last 7 sts on two stitch holders, leaving the remaining thirty-five stitches on your main knitting needle to be worked as follows:

Row 21   k2 tog mc, k9 mc, k1c1, k3 mc, k1c1, k1 mc, k1c1, k1 mc, k1c1, k3 mc, k1c1, k9 mc, k2 tog mc
Row 22   p2 tog mc, p7 mc, p1c1, p3 mc, p1c1, p2 mc, p1c1, p2 mc, p1c1, p3 mc, p1c1, p7 mc, p2 tog mc
Row 23   k2 tog mc, k9 mc, k1c1, k3 mc, k1c1, k3 mc, k1c1, k9 mc, k2 tog mc
Row 24   p9 mc, p1c1, p3 mc, p3c1, p3 mc, p1c1, p9 mc
Row 25   k8 mc, k1c1, k3 mc, k1c1, k1 mc, k1c1, k1 mc, k1c1, k3 mc, k1c1, k8 mc

m1 at beg and end, including these, work as follows:

Row 26   p12 mc, p1c1, p1 mc, p1c1, p1 mc, p1c1, p1 mc, p1c1, p12 mc

m1 at beg and end, including these, work as follows:

Row 27   k15 mc, k1c1, k1 mc, k1c1, k15 m

m1 at beg and end k, including these, work as follows:

Row 28   K35 mc

Hold this work on needle, and working first on the rs 7 sts on our stitch holder, place these 7 sts on to a 4 mm knitting needle, working rows as follows:

Row 21   k5, k2 tog
Row 22   p2 tog, p4
Row 23   k3, k2 tog
Row 24   p
Row 25   k
Row 26   m1 at beg in p   (5 sts)
Row 27   m1 at end in k   (6 sts)
Row 28   m1 at beg in p   (7 sts)

Place back on to stitch holder.

Now we will work the other 7 sts, working rs.

Row 21   k2 tog, k5
Row 22   p4, p2 tog
Row 23   k2 tog, k3
Row 24   p
Row 25   k
Row 26   m1 at end in p   (5 sts)
Row 27   m1 at beg in k   (6 sts)
Row 28   m1 at end in p   (7 sts)

Now we join all three parts together, totalling 49 sts.

Row 29   k
Row 30   p
Row 31   k
Row 32   p
Row 33   *k5, k2 tog, *r
Row 34   p

Change to c1, leaving a nice eight inches of mc yarn to sew up with later.

Row 35   *k5, k2 tog, *r
Row 36   p
Row 37   *k2 tog, yfwd, k1, *r
Row 38   p
Row 39   k
Row 40   p

B/o   Leave approximately four inches of c1 to sew up the neck area.

Mini Sleeves

C/o 20 sts on 4 mm knitting needles.

Row 1   k
Row 2   p
Row 3   k m1 at beg and end
Row 4   p m1 at beg and end

b/o

Repeat for second sleeve.

Tidy and sew sweater together.

Twilight

This sweater will be six inches in length.

Items you will need:

3¼ mm knitting needles
4 mm knitting needles
20 gm double knit yarn, two colours
Threading yarn needle
Scissors
Pencil and paper

C/o 38 sts, 3¼ mm knitting needles

Ribbing

Row 1   K2, p2
             r for three more rows
Change to 4 mm knitting needles.

Starting the Wave Pattern

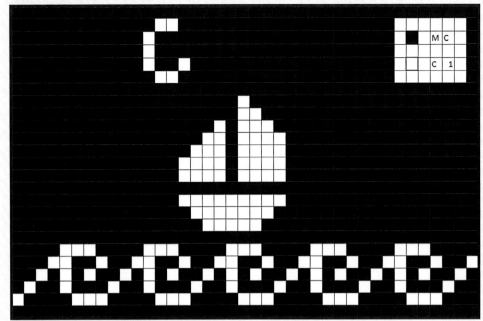

Increase first stitch to give 39 sts and k as follows:

Row 1   (RS) k3 mc, k3c1, k4 mc, k3c1, k4 mc, k3c1, k4 mc, k3c1, k4 mc, k3c1, k4 mc, k1c1

Row 2   (WS) p1 mc, p1c1, p2 mc, p1c1, p3 mc, p1c1, p2 mc, p1c1, p3 mc, p1c1, p2 mc, p1c1, p3 mc, p1c1, p2 mc, p1c1, p3 mc, p1c1, p2 mc, p1c1, p3 mc, p1c1, p2 mc

Row 3   k1 mc, k1c1, k2 mc, k1c1, k1 mc, k1c1, k1 mc, k1c1, k2 mc, k1c1, k1 mc,k1c1, k1 mc, k1c1, k2 mc, k1c1, k1 mc, k1c1, k1 mc, k1c1, k2 mc, k1c1, k1 mc,k1c1, k1 mc, k1c1, k2 mc, k1c1, k1 mc, k1c1, k1 mc, k1c1, k2 mc

Row 4   p3 mc, p2c1, p2 mc, p1c1, p2 mc, p2c1, p2 mc, p1c1, p2 mc, p2c1, p2 mc, p1c1, p2 mc, p2c1, p2 mc, p1c1, p2 mc, p2c1, p2 mc, p1c1, p2 mc, p1c1

Row 5   k4 mc, k3c1, k4 mc, k3c1, k4 mc, k3c1, k4 mc, k3c1, k4 mc, k3c1, k4 mc

Starting the boat Pattern

Row 6   p17 mc, p5 c1, p17 mc

m5 sts, including these, work as follows:

Row 7   k21 mc, k7c1, k16 mc

m5 sts, including these, work as follows:

Row 8   p20 mc, p9c1, p20 mc
Row 9   k24 mc, k1c1, k24 mc
Row 10   p20 mc, p4c1, p1 mc, p4c1, p20 mc
Row 11   k20 mc, k4c1, k1 mc, k4c1, k20 mc

Row 12	p21 mc, p3c1, p1 mc, p2c1, p1 mc, p1c1, p20 mc
Row 13	k20 mc, k4c1, k1 mc, k2c1, k22 mc
Row 14	p23 mc, p1c1, p1 mc, p3c1, p21 mc
Row 15	k22 mc, k2c1, k25 mc
Row 16	p25 mc, p1c1, p23 mc

Shape for Front Leg Holes

Hold the first and last 7 sts on two stitch holders, leaving the remaining thirty-five stitches on your main knitting needle to be worked as follows:

Row 17	k2 tog, k31, k2 tog
Row 18	p2 togmc, p9 mc, p2c1, p20 mc, p2 tog mc
Row 19	kt2 tog mc, k18 mc, k1c1, k2 mc, k1c1, k7 mc, k2 tog mc
Row 20	p8 mc, p1c1, p20 mc
Row 21	k20 mc, k1c1, k8 mc

m1 at beg and end, including these, work as follows:

Row 22	p10 mc, p2c1, p19 mc	(31 sts)

m1 at beg and end, including these, work as follows:

Row 23	k	(33 sts)

m1 at beg and end, including these, work as follows:

Row 24	p	(35 sts)

Hold this work on the needle, and working first on the rs 7 sts on our stitch holder, place these 7 sts on to a 4 mm knitting needle. Work rows as follows:

Row 17	k5, k2 tog	
Row 18	p2 tog, p4	
Row 19	k3, k2 tog	
Row 20	p	
Row 21	k	
Row 22	m1 at beg in p	(5 sts)
Row 23	m1 at end in k	(6 sts)
Row 24	m1 at beg in p	(7 sts)

Place back on to stitch holder.

Now, we will work the other 7 sts, working rs.

Row 17	k2 tog, k5	
Row 18	p4, p2 tog	
Row 19	k2 tog, k3	
Row 20	p	
Row 21	k	
Row 22	m1 at end in p	(5 sts)
Row 23	m1 at beg in k	(6 sts)
Row 24	m1 at end in p	(7 sts)

Now we join all three parts together, totalling 49 sts.

Row 25	k
Row 26	p

Repeat rows 25 and 26 for four more rows.

Row 31	*k5, k2 tog, *r, k1
Row 32	p
Row 33	*k5, k2 tog, *r, k1
Row 34	p

Change to 3¼ mm knitting needles.

Ribbing

Row 1	k2, p2

Repeat Row 1 three more times.

B/o, leaving enough yarn to sew the sweater together.

For this sweater, I have chosen to do barely-there sleeves. If you prefer to have different sleeves, then check out my page of sleeves.

Barely-there Sleeves

C/o 24 sts on 4 mm knitting needles.

Row 1	k
Row 2	k
B/o	

Repeat for second sleeve.

Paws

This sweater will be thirteen inches in length.

Items you will need:

3¼ mm knitting needles

4 mm knitting needles

100 gm chunky knit yarn, two colours

Threading yarn needle

Scissors

Pencil and paper

C/o 51 sts, 4 mm knitting needles

Starting   in c1 Yarn

Ribbing

Row 1   *k1 p1, *r
Row 2   *p1, k1, *r

Repeat rows 1 and 2 for eight more rows.

Change to mc.

Row 11   k
Row 12   p

Row 13   k
Row 14   p
Row 15   k17 mc, k3c1, k31 mc
Row 16   p30 mc, p5c1, p16 mc
Row 17   k15 mc, k7c1, k29 mc
Row 18   p29 mc, p7c1, p15 mc
Row 19   k15 mc, k7c1, k9 mc, k3c1, k17 mc
Row 20   p16 mc, p5c1, p9 mc, p5c1, p16 mc
Row 21   k14 mc, k2c1, k1 mc, k3c1, k1 mc, k2c1, k6 mc, k7c1, k15 mc
Row 22   p15 mc, p7c1, p6 mc, p2c1, p5 mc, p2c1, p14 mc
            m6 sts at the beginning of the row and including these, work as follows:
Row 23   k22 mc, k2c1, k1 mc, k2c1, k8 mc, k7c1, k15 mc
            m6 sts at the beginning of the row and including these, work as follows:
Row 24   p22 mc, p5c1, p9 mc, p2c1, p1 mc, p2c1, p22 mc
Row 25   k34 mc, k2c1, k1 mc, k3c1, k1 mc, k2c1, k20 mc
Row 26   p20 mc, p2c1, p5 mc, p2c1, p34 mc
Row 27   k36 mc, k2c1, k1 mc, k2c1, k22 mc
Row 28   p22 mc, p2c1, p1 mc, p2c1, p36 mc
Row 29   k23 mc, k3c1, k37 mc
Row 30   p36 mc, p5c1, p22 mc
Row 31   k21 mc, k7c1, k35 mc
Row 32   p35 mc, p7c1, p21 mc
Row 33   k21 mc, k7c1, k9 mc, k3c1, k23 mc
Row 34   p22 mc, p5c1, p9 mc, p5c1, p22 mc
Row 35   k20 mc, k2c1, k1 mc, k3c1, k1 mc, k2c1, k6 mc, k7c1, k21 mc
Row 36   p21 mc, p7c1, k6 mc, p2c1, p5 mc, p2c1, p20 mc
Row 37   k22 mc, k2c1, k1 mc, k2c1, k8 mc, k7c1, k21 mc
Row 38   p22 mc, p5c1, p9 mc, p2c1, p1 mc, p2c1, p22 mc
Row 39   k34 mc, k2c1, k1 mc, k3c1, k1 mc, k2c1, k20 mc
Row 40   p20 mc, p2c1, p5 mc, p2c1, p34 mc
Row 41   k36 mc, k2c1, k1 mc, k2c1, k22 mc
Row 42   p22 mc, p2c1, p1 mc, p2c1, p36 mc

Shape for Front Leg Holes

Hold the first and last 9 sts on two stitch holders, leaving the remaining 45 sts on your main knitting needle to be worked as follows:

Row 43   k2 tog, k41 k2 tog
Row 44   p2 tog, p39, p2 tog
Row 45   k2 tog, k37, k2 tog
Row 46   p

Row 47	k	
Row 48	p	
Row 49	k	
Row 50	p	
Row 51	k	
Row 52	m1 at beg and end in p	(41 sts)
Row 53	m1 at beg and end in k	(43 sts)
Row 54	m1 at beg and end in p	(45 sts)

Hold this work on needle, and working first on the rs 9 sts on our stitch holder, place these 9 sts on to a 4 mm knitting needle. Work rows as follows:

Row 43	k7, k2 tog	
Row 44	p2 tog, p6	
Row 45	k5, k2 tog	
Row 46	p	
Row 47	k	
Row 48	p	
Row 49	k	
Row 50	p	
Row 51	k	
Row 52	m1 at beg in p	7 sts
Row 53	m1 at end in k	8 sts
Row 54	m1 at beg in p	9 sts

Place back on to stitch holder.

Now we will work the other 7 sts working rs.

Row 43	k2 tog, k7	
Row 44	p6, p2 tog	
Row 45	k2 tog, k5	
Row 46	p	
Row 47	k	
Row 48	p	
Row 49	k	
Row 50	p	
Row 51	k	
Row 52	m1 at end in p	7 sts
Row 53	m1 at beg in k	8 sts
Row 54	m1 at end in p	9 sts

Now we join all three parts together, totalling 63 sts.

Row 55   k
Row 56   p
             r rows 5533 and 5634 for six more rows
Row 63   *k5, k2 tog, *r
Row 64   p
Row 65   *k5, k2 tog, *r, k5
Row 66   p
Row 67   k
Row 68   p
Row 69   k
             Change to c1, leaving enough mc yarn to sew up the sweater with later.
Row 70   p

Ribbing

Row 71   *k1, p1, *r
Row 72   *p1, k1, *r

Repeat rows 71 & 72 for eight more rows.

b/o   Leave approximately four inches of c1 to sew up the neck area.

Cone Sleeves

On 4 mm knitting needles, c/o 20 sts in c1.

Row 1   *k2, p2, *r
Row 2   *p2, k2, *r

Change to mc

Row 3   k
Row 4   p
Row 5   k4, m1 (and k it), k12, m1 (and k it), k4
Row 6   p
Row 7   k4, m1 (and k it), k12, m1 (and k it), k4
Row 8   p
Row 9   k4, m1 (and k it), k12, m1 (and k it), k4
Row 10   p
Row 11   k
Row 12   p

b/o

Repeat for second sleeve.

Knitted Bone Toy

Items you will need:

4 mm knitting needles
15 gm double knit yarn
Threading yarn needle
Scissors
Toy filling
Pencil and paper

C/o 3 sts

Row 1   k

C/o 3 sts

Row 1   k

Place all 6 sts on to one 4 mm knitting needle.

Row 2   in p increase m1 each end and m1 in the middle(9 sts)
Row 3   k
Row 4   p

Row 5	in k decrease I st each end	(7 sts)
Row 6	in p decrease I st each end	(5 sts)
Row 7	k	
Row 8	p	

Repeat rows 7 and 8 for the next eight rows

Row 17	in k mI each end	(7 sts)
Row 18	in p mI each end	(9 sts)
Row 19	k	
Row 20	p	
Row 21	in k decrease I st each end and I st in the middle	(6 sts)
Row 22	p 3 sts turn	

b/o cut yarn

Reattach yarn and p last 3 sts turn.

b/o cut yarn.

Assembling the Bone

Sew the bone together inside out. When you have an inch left, turn right way out, stuff with toy filling till the right shape is achieved. Sew the remaining inch together, knot yarn, then thread the yarn into the main body of the bone. Pull out the other side and cut the yarn. The yarn should disappear inside the bone, leaving no unsightly ends.

Flutterby

This sweater will be nine inches in length (not including neck).

Items you will need:

5 mm knitting needles
4 mm knitting needles
55 gm chunky knit yarn, two colours
Threading yarn needle
Scissors
Pencil and paper

On 4 mm knitting needles, c/o 47 sts.

Ribbing

Row 1   *k1, p1, *r
Row 2   *p1, k1, *r

Repeat these two rows for six more rows.

Change to 5 mm knitting needles.

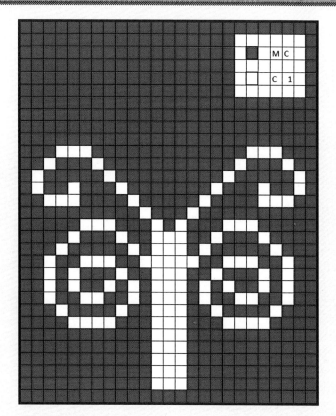

	M C
	C 1

Row 9   k22 mc, k3c1, k22 mc
Row 10   p22 mc, p3c1, p22 mc

Repeat these two rows three more times.

Row 14   p15 mc, p4c1, p3 mc, p3c1, p3 mc, p4c1, p15 mc

Increase five stitches at the beginning of the row, then k as follows:

Row 15   k19 mc, k1c1, k4 mc, k1c1, k2 mc, k3c1, k2 mc, k1c1, k4 mc, k1c1, k14 mc

Increase five stitches at the beginning of the row, then p as follows:

Row 16   p18 mc, p1c1, p2 mc, p2c1, p2 mc, p1c1, p1 mc, p3c1, p1 mc, p1c1, p2 mc, p2c1, p2 mc, p1c1, p18 mc
Row 17   k18 mc, k1c1, k1 mc, k1c1, k2 mc, k1c1, k1 mc, k1c1, k1 mc, k3c1, k1 mc, k1c1, k1 mc, k1c1, k2 mc, k1c1, k1 mc, k1c1, k18 mc
Row 18   p18 mc, p1c1, p1 mc, p1c1, p3 mc, p1c1, p2 mc, p3c1, p2 mc, p1c1, p3 mc, p1c1, p1 mc, p1c1, p18 mc
Row 19   k18 mc, k1c1, k2 mc, k3c1, k2 mc, k5c1, k2 mc, k3c1, k2 mc, k1c1, k18 mc
Row 20   p19 mc, p1c1, p5 mc, p1c1, p1 mc, p3c1, p1 mc, p1c1, p5 mc, p1c1, p19 mc
Row 21   k20 mc, k1c1, k3 mc, k1c1, k2 mc, k3c1, k2 mc, k1c1, k3 mc, k1c1, k20 mc
Row 22   p21 mc, p3c1, p3 mc, p1c1, p1 mc, p1c1, p3 mc, p3c1, p21 mc
Row 23   k26 mc, k1c1, k3 mc, k1c1, k26 mc
Row 24   p18 mc, p3c1, p4 mc, p1c1, p5 mc, p1c1, p4 mc, p3c1, p18 mc

Shaping for Front Leg Holes

Hold the first and last 8 sts on two stitch holders, leaving the remaining 41 sts on your main knitting needle to be worked as follows:

Row 25	k2 togmc, k7 mc, k1c1, k2 mc, k1c1, k3 mc, k1c1, k7 mc, k1c1, k3 mc, k1c1, k2 mc, k1c1, k7 mc, k2 togmc	(39 sts)
Row 26	p2 togmc, p6 mc, p1c1, p5 mc, p1c1, p9 mc, p1c1, p5 mc, p1c1, p6 mc, p2 togmc	(37 sts)
Row 27	k2 togmc, k6 mc, k1c1, k3 mc, k1c1, k11 mc, k1c1, k3 mc, k1c1, k6 mc, k2 togmc	(35 sts)
Row 28	p8 mc, p3c1, p13 mc, p3c1, p8 mc	
Row 29	k	
Row 30	p	
Row 31	k	
Row 32	m1 at beg and end in p	(37 sts)
Row 33	m1 at beg and end in k	(39 sts)
Row 34	m1 at beg and end in p	(41 sts)

Hold this work on needle (41 sts), and working first on the rs 8 sts on our stitch holder, place these 8 sts on to a 4 mm knitting needle. Work rows as follows:

Row 25	k6, k2 tog	
Row 26	p2 tog, p5	
Row 27	k4, k2 tog	
Row 28	p	
Row 29	k	
Row 30	p	
Row 31	k	
Row 32	m1 at beg in p	6 sts
Row 33	m1 at end in k	7 sts
Row 34	m1 at beg in p	8 sts

Place back on to stitch holder.

Now we will work the other 8 sts, working rs.

Row 25	k2 tog, k6
Row 26	p5, p2 tog
Row 27	k2 tog, k4
Row 28	p
Row 29	k

Row 30	p	
Row 31	k	
Row 32	m1 at end in p	6 sts
Row 33	m1 at beg in k	7 sts
Row 34	m1 at end in p	8 sts

Now we join all three parts together, totalling 57 sts.

Row 35	k
Row 36	p

Repeat these two rows eight more times.

Row 45	*k5, k2 tog, *r, k5, s1 (slip 1 stitch), k2 tog, psso
Row 46	p
Row 47	*k5, k2 tog, *r, k6
Row 48	p

Change to 4 mm knitting needles.

Ribbing

Row 1	*k1, p1, *r
Row 2	*p1, k1, *r

Repeat rows 1 and 2 for eight more rows.

B/o, leaving enough yarn for sewing together.

Barely-there Sleeves

C/o 28 sts on 4 mm knitting needles.

Row 1	k
Row 2	k

B/o

Sew sweater together (see page 11 for details).

Little Rabbit

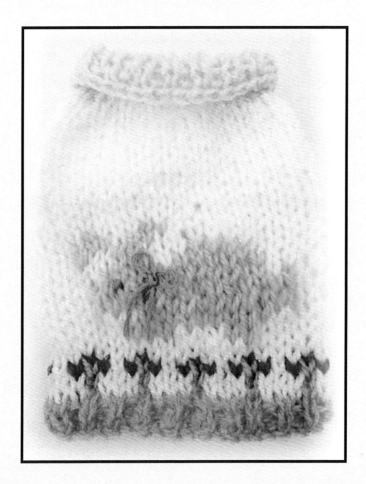

Length 4″

The sweater photographed is four inches in length.

Items you will need:

3¼ mm knitting needles
4 mm knitting needles
20 gm double knit yarn
Threading yarn needle
Sewing needle
Scissors
Pencil and paper

With 3¼ mm needles, cast on thirty-three stitches.

For the next two rows, work the waist ribbing.

Row 1   RS *k1, p1 *r
Row 2   WS *p1, k1 *r

Now change to 4 mm needles and work in stst.

Pattern starts:

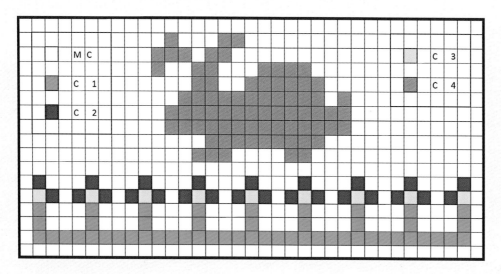

Row 3	(RS) *K1c1, k3 mc, *r
Row 4	(WS) * P1c1, p3 mc, *r
Row 5	k1c2, k1c3, k1 mc, k1c3, k1c2, k1c3, k1 mc, k1c3, k1c2, k1c3, k1 mc, k1c3, k1c2, k1c3, k1 mc, K1c3, k1c2, k1c3, k1 mc, k1c3, k1c2, k1c3, k1 mc, k1c3, k1c2, k1c3, k1 mc, k1c3, k1c2, k1c3, k1 mc, k1c3, k1c2
Row 6	p1c3, p3 mc, p1c3, p3 mc, p1c3, p3 mc, p1c3, p3 mc, p1c3, p3 mc, p1c3, p3 mc, p1c3, p3 mc, p1c3, p3 mc, p1c1,
Row 7	k
Row 8	p12 mc, p3c4, p4 mc, p2c4, p12 mc
	m4 sts at beg, including these, work as follows: (37 sts)
Row 9	k15 mc, k9c4, k13 mc

m4 sts at beg, including these, work as follows: (41 sts)

Row 10	p14 mc, p14c4, p13 mc
Row 11	k13 mc, k14c4, k14 mc
Row 12	p15 mc, p11c4, p1 mc, p1c4, p13 mc
Row 13	k15 mc, k6c4, k2 mc, k2c4, k16 mc
Row 14	p13 mc, p1c4, p2 mc, p2c4, p3 mc, p4c4, p16 mc

Shaping the Leg Holes (Back)

Take the first 7 sts and place on a stitch holder. Leave enough yarn attached to knit up later and cut. Then cut approximately fifty-five inches of yarn to use later on the other arm hole.

Row 15	k2t k13 mc, k2c4, k1 mc, k3c4, k4 mc, k2tmc, place the remaining 7 st on stitch holder.
Row 16	p2tmc, p4 mc, p1c4, p3 mc, p2c4, p11 mc, p2tmc

Row 17	k2t k19 k2t	
Row 18	p	
Row 19	k	
Row 20	in p m1 at beg and end	(23 sts)
Row 21	in k m1 at beg and end	(25 sts)
Row 22	in p m1 at beg and end	(27 sts)
	cut yarn	

Shaping the Arm Holes (Sides)

Take the 7 sts on the rs and put back on to the 4 mm knitting needle. With the yarn we left on these stitches, we begin shaping:

Row 15	k5 k2t (rs)	
Row 16	p2t p4 (ws)	
Row 17	k3 k2t	
Row 18	p	
Row 19	k	
Row 20	p m1 at beg	(5 sts)
Row 21	k m1 at end	(6 sts)
Row 22	p m1 at beg	(7 sts)

Take the other 7 sts on the stitch holder and put back on to the 4 mm knitting needle. With the yarn we cut earlier, we work these stitches. We begin shaping the second arm hole.

Row 15	k2t k5 (rs)	
Row 16	p4 p2t (ws)	
Row 17	k2t k3	
Row 18	p	
Row 19	k	
Row 20	p m1 at end	(5 sts)
Row 21	k m1 at beg	(6 sts)
Row 22	p m1 at end	(7 sts)

Now attach the main yarn and we join all the three parts.

Row 23	rs k (as you knit across, tie off loose ends to working yarn)
Row 24	ws p

Continue in stst for another two rows.

Row 27	*k5 k2t *r, k6
	Change to blue yarn then.
Row 28	p

Ribbing

Change to 3¼ mm knitting needles.

Row 1   *k1 p1 *r
Row 2   *p1 k1 *r

Repeat these two rows four more times.

B/o leave enough yarn to sew sweater up.

Barely-there Sleeves

On 3¼ mm knitting needles, c/o 22 sts.

Row 1 k
Row 2 k

b/o

Repeat for the second sleeve.

Bunny

This sweater will be twelve inches in length (not including neck).

Items you will need:

3¼ mm knitting needles

4 mm knitting needles

50 gm double knit yarn, two colours

Threading yarn needle

Pom-pom

Googly eyes

Scissors

Pencil and paper

On 3¼ mm knitting needles, c/o 53 sts.

Ribbing

Row 1   RS *k1, p1, *r
Row 2   WS *p1, k1, *r

Repeat these two rows for eight more rows.

Change to 4 mm knitting needles.

Row 11   k
Row 12   p

Repeat these two rows four more times.

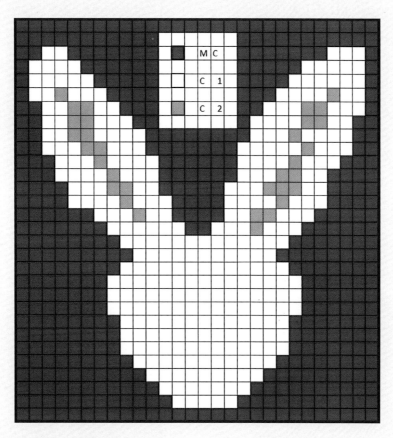

Row 17   k24 mc, k5c1, k24 mc
Row 18   p23 mc, p7c1, p23 mc
Row 19   k22 mc, k9c1, k22 mc
Row 20   p21 mc, p11c1, p21 mc
Row 21   k20 mc, k13c1, k20 mc
Row 22   p20 mc, p13c1, p20 mc
Row 23   k20 mc, k13c1, k20 mc
Row 24   p19 mc, p15c1, p19 mc
Row 25   k19 mc, k15c1, k19 mc
Row 26   p19 mc, p15c1, p19 mc
                m5 stitches at the beginning of the row, including these, work as follows:
Row 27   k25 mc, k13c1, k20 mc
                m5 stitches at the beginning of the row, including these, work as follows:

Row 28   p26 mc, p11c1, p26 mc

Row 29   k25 mc, k13c1, k25 mc

Row 30   p24 mc, p6c1, p2 mc, p3c1, p1c2, p3c1, p24 mc

Row 31   k23 mc, k3c1, k2c2, k2c1, k4 mc, k2c1, k1c2, k3c1, k23 mc

Row 32   p21 mc, p4c1, p1c2, p3c1, p4 mc, p4c1, p1c2, p3c1, p22 mc

Row 33   k22 mc, k2c1, k3c2, k3c1, k5 mc, k2c1, k2c2, k3c1, k21 mc

Row 34   p20 mc, p4c1, p1c2, p3c1, p6 mc, p3c1, p2c2, p2c1, p22 mc

Row 35   k21 mc, k3c1, k1c2, k4c1, k6 mc, k4c1, k1c2, k3c1, k20 mc

Row 36   p19 mc, p3c1, p2c2, p3c1, p7 mc, p5c1, p1c2, p3c1, p20 mc

Row 37   k20 mc, k4c1, k1c2, k3c1, k8 mc, k4c1, k2c2, k2c1, k19 mc

Row 38   p19 mc, p2c1, p2c2, p3c1, p9 mc, p4c1, p2c2, p2c1, p20 mc

Row 39   k19 mc, k3c1, k2c2, k3c1, k11 mc, k2c1, k2c2, k2c1, k19 mc

Row 40   p18 mc, p2c1, p1c2, p3c1, p13 mc, p4c1, p1c2, p2c1, p19 mc

Row 41   k19 mc, k6c1, k15 mc, k5c1, k18 mc

Row 42   p18 mc, p4c1, p17 mc, p5c1, p19 mc

Row 43   k19 mc, k3c1, k20 mc, k2c1, k19 mc

Row 44   p

Shaping for Front Leg Holes

Hold the first and last 9 sts on two stitch holders, leaving the remaining forty-five stitches on your main knitting needle to be worked as follows:

Row 45   k2 tog, k41, k2 tog

Row 46   p2 tog, p39, p2 tog

Row 47   k2 tog, k37, k2 tog

Row 48   p

Row 49   k

Row 50   p

Row 51   k

Row 52   m1 at beg and end in p   (37 sts)

Row 53   m1 at beg and end in k   (39 sts)

Row 54   m1 at beg and end in p   (41 sts)

Hold this work on needle (41 sts), and working first on the rs 9 sts on our stitch holder, place these 9 sts on to a 4 mm knitting needle. Work rows as follows:

Row 45   k7, k2 tog

Row 46   p2 tog, p6

Row 47   k5, k2 tog

Row 48	p	
Row 49	k	
Row 50	p	
Row 51	k	
Row 52	m1 at beg in p	7 sts
Row 53	m1 at end in k	8 sts
Row 54	m1 at beg in p	9 sts

Place back on to stitch holder.

Now we will work the other 9 sts, working rs.

Row 45	k2 tog, k7	
Row 46	p6, p2 tog	
Row 47	k2 tog, k5	
Row 48	p	
Row 49	k	
Row 50	p	
Row 51	k	
Row 52	m1 at end in p	7 sts
Row 53	m1 at beg in k	8 sts
Row 54	m1 at end in p	9 sts

Now we join all three parts together, totalling 63 sts.

| Row 55 | k |
| Row 66 | p |

Repeat these two rows twelve more times.

Row 79	k1, *k9, k2 tog, *r, k5, k2 tog
Row 80	p
Row 81	k2, *k7, k2 tog, *r, k1
Row 82	p

Change to 3¼ mm knitting needles.

Ribbing

| Row 1 | *k1, p1, *r |
| Row 2 | *p1, k1, *r |

Repeat rows 1 and 2 for eight more rows.

B/o, leaving enough yarn for sewing together.

Short Sleeves

On 3¼ mm knitting needles, c/o your required number of sts.

Row 1   *k1, p1, *r
Row 2   *p1, k1, *r

Change to 4 mm knitting needles.

Row 3   k
Row 4   p
Row 5   *m1 stitch and k, k7, *r, k3
Row 6   p

B/o

Sew sweater together (see page 11 for details).

Hug-me Hoodie

This sweater will be six inches in length (not including ribbed neck).

Items you will need:

3¼ mm knitting needles
4 mm knitting needles
30 gm double knit yarn, two colours
Threading yarn needle
Pom-pom
Scissors
Pencil and paper

On 3¼ mm knitting needles c/o 39 sts c1.

Ribbing

Row 1   RS *k1, p1, *r
Row 2   WS *p1, k1, *r

Repeat these two rows for two more rows.

Change to 4 mm knitting needles. Change to mc and work as follows:

Row 5   k
Row 6   p

Repeat these two rows four more times.

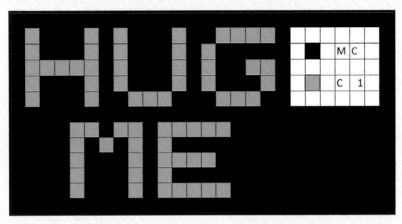

Me Pattern (row 11–15) Hug Pattern (row 17–21>

m5 stitches at the beginning of the row, including these, work as follows:

Row 11   k19 mc, k5c1, k1 mc, k1c1, k3 mc, k1c1, k14 mc
               m5 stitches at the beginning of the row, including these, work as follows:
Row 12   p19 mc, p1c1, p3 mc, p1c1, p1 mc, p1c1, p23 mc
Row 13   k15 mc, k4c1, k1 mc, k1c1, k3 mc, k1c1, k19 mc
Row 14   p19 mc,* p1c1, p1 mc, *r, p23 mc
Row 15   k19 mc, k5c1, k14 mc, k2c1, k1 mc, k2c1, k19 mc
Row 16   p
Row 17   k17 mc, k3c1, k3 mc, k3c1, k2 mc, k1c1, k3 mc, k1c1, k16 mc
Row 18   p16 mc, p1c1, p3 mc, p1c1, p1 mc, p1c1, p3 mc, p1c1, p1 mc, p1c1, p3 mc, p1c1, p16 mc
Row 19   k16 mc, k2c1, k2 mc, k1c1, k1 mc, k1c1, k3 mc, k1c1, k1 mc, k5c1, k16 mc
Row 20   p16 mc, p1c1, p3 mc, p1c1, p1 mc, p1c1, p3 mc, p1c1, p1 mc, p1c1, p20 mc
Row 21   k16 mc, k4c1, k2 mc, k1c1, k3 mc, k1c1, k1 mc, k1c1, k3 mc, k1c1, k16 mc
Row 22   p

Shaping for Front Leg Holes

Hold the first and last 7 sts on two stitch holders, leaving the remaining thirty-five stitches on your main knitting needle to be worked as follows:

Row 23   k2 tog, k31, k2 tog
Row 24   p2 tog, p29, p2 tog

Row 25   k2 tog, k27, k2 tog
Row 26   p
Row 27   k
Row 28   m1 st each end in p   (31 sts)
Row 29   m1 st each end in k   (33 sts)
Row 30   m1 st each end in p   (35 sts)

Hold this work on needle (35 sts), and working first on the rs 7 sts on our stitch holder, place these 7 sts on to a 4 mm knitting needle. Work rows as follows:

Row 23   k5, k2 tog
Row 24   p2 tog, p4
Row 25   k3, k2 tog
Row 26   p
Row 27   k
Row 28   m1 at beg in p   5 sts
Row 29   m1 at end in k   6 sts
Row 30   m1 at beg in p   7 sts

Place back on to stitch holder.

Now we will work the other 7 sts, working rs.

Row 23   k2 tog, k5
Row 24   p4, p2 tog
Row 25   k2 tog, k3
Row 26   p
Row 27   k
Row 28   m1 at end in p   5 sts
Row 29   m1 at beg in k   6 sts
Row 30   m1 at end in p   7 sts

Now, we join all three parts together.

Row 31   k
Row 32   p
           Repeat these two rows four more times.

Row 37   *k5, k2 tog, *r,
Row 38   p
Row 39   *k5, k2 tog, *r
Row 40   p

Change to c1.

Working in garter st now.

| Row 41 | k |
| Row 42 | k |

Repeat rows 1 and 2 for two more rows.

Knitting the Hood

Row 45	working in k, b/o the first and last four stitches
Row 46	k4c1, p19 mc, k4c1
Row 47	k4c1, k19 mc, k4c1
Row 48	k4c1, p19 mc, k4c1
	Repeat rows 47 and 48 for fifteen more rows.

b/o in p

Long Sleeves

On 3¼ mm knitting needles, c/o 18 sts.

| Row 1 | *k1, p1, *r |
| Repeat Row 1 for three more rows. |

Row 5	k
Row 6	p
Row 7	*k6, m1, *r
Row 8	p
Row 9	k6, m1, k8, m1, k6
Row 10	p
Row 11	k4, m1, k14, m1, k4
Row 12	p

b/o

Sew sweater together (see page 11 for details).

Reindeer

This sweater will be eight inches in length.

Items you will need:

3¼ mm knitting needles

4 mm knitting needles

Googly eyes

Red pom-pom

30 g double knit yarn, two colours

Threading yarn needle

Scissors

Pencil and paper

C/o 44 sts 3¼ mm knitting needles c1.

Ribbing

Row 1   k1, p1

Row 2   k1, p1

               R for four more rows.

Change to 4 mm knitting needles and mc.

Row 7   k
Row 8   p
               R for two more rows.

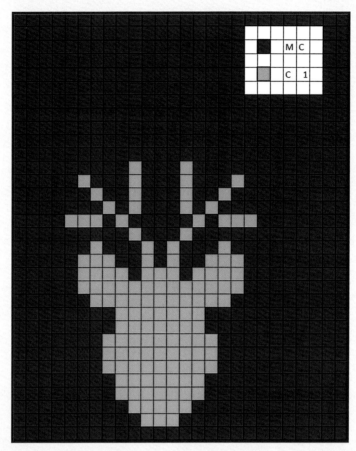

Increase first stitch to give 45 sts and k as follows:

Row 11   k21 mc, k3c1, k21 mc
Row 12   p20 mc, p5c1, p20 mc
Row 13   k19 mc, k7c1, k19 mc
Row 14   p19 mc, p7c1, p19 mc

Increase 5 sts, including these k, as follows:

Row 15   k23 mc, k9c1, k18 mc

Increase 5 sts, including these p, as follows:

Row 16   p23 mc, p9c1, p23 mc
Row 17   k23 mc, k9c1, k23 mc
Row 18   p24 mc, p7c1, p24 mc
Row 19   k24 mc, k7c1, k24 mc

Row 20   p22 mc, p11cl, p22 mc
Row 21   k21 mc, k13cl, k21 mc
Row 22   p21 mc, p4cl, p1 mc, p3cl, p1 mc, p4cl, p21 mc
Row 23   k21 mc, k3cl, k2 mc, k1cl, k1 mc, k1cl, k2 mc, k3cl, k21 mc
Row 24   p20 mc, p1cl, p3 mc, p1cl, p1 mc, p1cl, p3 mc, p1cl, p20 mc
Row 25   k26 mc, k1cl, k1 mc, k1cl, k26 mc
Row 26   p20 mc, p4cl, p1 mc, p1cl, p3 mc, p1cl, p1 mc, p4cl, p20 mc
Row 27   k24 mc, k1cl, k5 mc, k1cl, k24 mc
Row 28   p23 mc, p1cl, p1 mc, p1cl, p3 mc, p1cl, p1 mc, p1cl, p23 mc

Shape for Front Leg Holes

Hold the first and last 7 sts on two stitch holders, leaving the remaining forty-one stitches on your main knitting needle to be worked as follows:

Row 29   k2 togmc, k13 mc, k1cl, k2 mc, k1cl, k3 mc, k1cl, k2 mc, k1cl, k13 mc k2 togmc

Row 30   p2 togmc, p11 mc, p1cl, p3 mc, p1cl, p3 mc, p1cl, p3 mc, p1cl, p11 mc p2 togmc

Row 31   k2 togmc, k14 mc, k1cl, k3 mc, k1cl, k14 mc, k2 togmc   (35 sts)
Row 32   p
Row 33   k
Row 34   p
Row 35   k
            M1 at beg and end, including these, work as follows:
Row 36   p   (37 sts)
            M1 at beg and end, including these, work as follows:
Row 37   k   (39 sts)
M1 at beg and end, including these, work as follows:
Row 38   p   (41 sts)

Hold this work on needle, and working first on the rs 7 sts on our stitch holder, place these 7 sts on to a 4 mm knitting needle. Work rows as follows:

Row 29   k5, k2 tog
Row 30   p2 tog, p4
Row 31   k3, k2 tog
Row 32   p
Row 33   k
Row 34   p

Row 35	k	
Row 36	m1 at beg in p,	(5 sts)
Row 37	m1 at end in k,	(6 sts)
Row 38	m1 at beg in p,	(7 sts)

Place back on to stitch holder.

Now we will work the other 7 sts, working rs.

Row 29	k2 tog, k5	
Row 30	p4, p2 tog	
Row 31	k2 tog, k3	
Row 32	p	
Row 33	k	
Row 34	p	
Row 35	k	
Row 36	m1 at end in p	(5 sts)
Row 37	m1 at beg in k	(6 sts)
Row 38	m1 at end in p	(7 sts)

Join all three parts together, totalling 55 sts.

Row 39	k
Row 40	p

Repeat rows 25 and 26 for six more rows.

Row 47	k1, *k5, k2 tog, *r, k1
Row 48	p
Row 49	*k5, k2 tog, *r, k1
Row 50	p

Change to 3¼ mm knitting needles.

Ribbing

Row 1	k1, p1
Row 2	p1, k1

Repeat row 1 and 2 four more times.

b/o, leaving enough yarn to sew the sweater together.

Medium Sleeves

On 3¼ mm knitting needles, c/o 20 sts.

Row 1   *k1, p1, *r
Row 2   *k1, p1, *r

Change to 4 mm knitting needles.

Row 3   k
Row 4   p
Row 5   k
Row 6   p
Row 7   k m1 at beg and end
Row 8   p
Row 9   k m1 at beg and end
Row 10   p

b/o

Pirate

This sweater will be six inches in length.

Items you will need:

3¼ mm knitting needles

4 mm knitting needles

20 gm double knit yarn, two colours

Threading yarn needle

Scissors

Pencil and paper

C/o 39 sts 3¼ mm knitting needles.

Ribbing

Row 1   K1, p1

Row 2   p1, k1

                Do this for two more rows.

Change to 4 mm knitting needles.

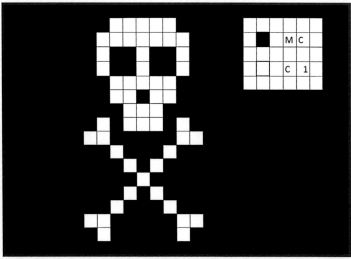

Row 5	(rs) k16 mc, k1c1, k5 mc, k1c1, k16 mc
Row 6	(ws) p15 mc, p2c1, p5 mc, p2c1, p15 mc
Row 7	k17 mc, k1c1, k3 mc, k1c1, k17 mc
Row 8	p18 mc, p1c1, p1 mc, p1c1, p18 mc
Row 9	k19 mc, k1c1, k19 mc
Row 10	p18 mc, p1c1, p1 mc, p1c1, p18 mc

At the start of Row 11, increase 5 sts, including these sts k as follows:

Row 11	k22 mc, k1c1, k3 mc, k1c1, k17 mc

At the start of Row 12, increase by 5 sts, including these sts p as follows:

Row 12	p20 mc, p2c1, p5 mc, p2c1, p20 mc
Row 13	k21 mc, k1c1, k1 mc, k3c1, k1 mc, k1c1, k21 mc
Row 14	p23 mc, p3c1, p23 mc
Row 15	k22 mc, k2c1, k1 mc, k2c1, k22 mc
Row 16	p22 mc, p5c1, p22 mc
Row 17	k21 mc, k1c1, k2 mc, k1c1, k2 mc, k1c1, k21 mc
Row 18	p21 mc, p1c1, p2 mc, p1c1, p2 mc, p1c1, p21 mc
Row 19	k21 mc, k7c1, k21 mc
Row 20	p22 mc, p5c1, p22 mc

Shape for Front Leg Holes

Hold the first and last 7 sts on two stitch holders, leaving the remaining thirty-five stitches on your main knitting needle to be worked as follows:

Row 21	k2 tog, k31, k2 tog
Row 22	p2 togmc, p29, p2 tog
Row 23	kt2 tog, k27, k2 tog
Row 24	p

Row 25   k
           m1 at beg and end, including these, work as follows:
Row 26   p
           m1 at beg and end, including these, work as follows:
Row 27   k
           m1 at beg and end, including these, work as follows:
Row 28   p

Hold this work on the needle, and working first on the rs 7 sts on our stitch holder, place these 7 sts on to a 4 mm knitting needle. Work rows as follows:

Row 21   k5, k2 tog
Row 22   p2 tog, p4
Row 23   k3, k2 tog
Row 24   p
Row 25   k
Row 26   m1 at beg in p   5sts
Row 27   m1 at end in k   6sts
Row 28   m1 at beg in p   7sts

Place back on to stitch holder.

Now we will work the other 7 sts, working rs.

Row 21   k2 tog, k5
Row 22   p4, p2 tog
Row 23   k2 tog, k3
Row 24   p
Row 25   k
Row 26   m1 at end in p   5sts
Row 27   m1 at beg in k   6sts
Row 28   m1 at end in p   7sts

Now we join all three parts together, totalling 49 sts.

Row 29   k
Row 30   p

Repeat rows 29 and 30 for four more rows.

Row 35   *k5, k2 tog, *r
Row 36   p
Row 37   *k5, k2 tog, *r

Row 38   p

Change to 3¼ mm knitting needles.

Ribbing

Row 19   k1, p1

Repeat Row 1 three more times.

b/o

b/o, leaving enough yarn to sew the sweater together.

Barely there sleeves

On 4 mm knitting needles, c/o 26 sts.

Row 1   k
Row 2   k

b/o

Spider

This sweater will be eight inches in length.

Items you will need:

3¼ mm knitting needles

4 mm knitting needles

Googly eyes

30 gm double knit yarn, two colours

Threading yarn needle

Scissors

Pencil and paper

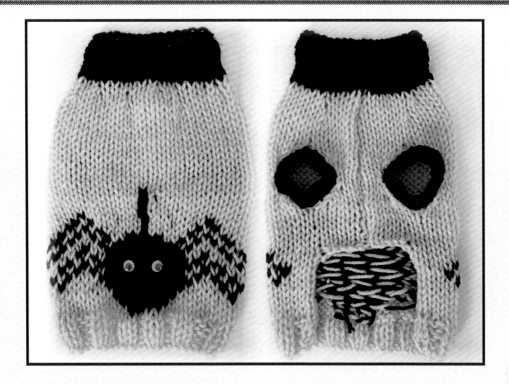

C/o 45 sts 3¼ mm knitting needles c1.

Ribbing

Row 1   k1, p1
Row 2   k1, p1
             r for four more rows.

Change to 4 mm knitting needles and mc.

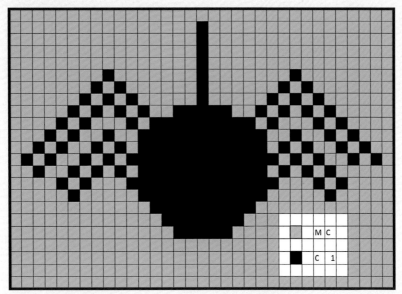

Row 7   k20 mc, k5c1, k20 mc
Row 8   p19 mc, p7c1, p19 mc
Row 9   k18 mc, k9c1, k18 mc

Row 10   p11 mc, p1c1, p5 mc, p11c1, p5 mc, p11c1
Row 11   k10 mc, k1c1, k1 mc, k1c1, k3 mc, k13c1, k3 mc, k1c1, k1 mc, k1c1, k10 mc
Row 12   p8 mc, p1c1, p2 mc, p1c1, p1 mc, p1c1, p1 mc, p1c1, p1 mc, p11c1, p1 mc, p1c1, p1 mc, p1c1, p1 mc, p1c1, p2 mc, p1c1, p8 mc
Row 13   k7 mc, k1c1, k1 mc, k1c1, k2 mc, k1c1, k1 mc, k1c1, k1 mc, k13c1, k1 mc, k1c1, k1 mc, k1c1, k2 mc, k1c1, k1 mc, k1c1, k7 mc
Row 14   p8 mc, p1c1, p1 mc, p1c1, p2 mc, p1c1, p1 mc, p1c1, p1 mc, p11c1, p1 mc, p1c1, p1 mc, p1c1, p2 mc, p1c1, p1 mc, p1c1, p8 mc

Increase 5 sts, including these, k as follows:

Row 15   k14 mc, k1c1, k1 mc, k1c1, k2 mc, k1c1, k2 mc, k11c1, k2 mc, k1c1, k2 mc, k1c1, k1 mc, k1c1, k14 mc

Increase 5 sts, including these, p as follows:

Row 16   p15 mc, p1c1, p1 mc, p1c1, p3 mc, p1c1, p1 mc, p9c1, p1 mc, p1c1, p3 mc, p1c1, p1 mc, p1c1, p15 mc
Row 17   k16 mc, k1c1, k1 mc, k1c1, k1 mc, k1c1, k1 mc, k1c1, k2 mc, k5c1, k2 mc, k1c1, k1 mc, k1c1, k1 mc, k1c1, k1 mc, k1c1, k16 mc
Row 18   p17 mc, p1c1, p1 mc, p1c1, p1 mc, p1c1, p5 mc, p1c1, p5 mc, p1c1, p1 mc, p1c1, p1 mc, p1c1, p17 mc
Row 19   k18 mc, k1c1, k1 mc, k1c1, k6 mc, k1c1, k6 mc, k1c1, k1 mc, k1c1, k18 mc
Row 20   p19 mc, p1c1, p7 mc, p1c1, p7 mc, p1c1, p19 mc
Row 21   k27 mc, k1c1, k27 mc
Row 22   p27 mc, p1c1, p27 mc
Row 23   k27 mc, k1c1, k27 mc
Row 24   p27 mc, p1c1, p27 mc
Row 25   k
Row 26   p
Row 27   k
Row 28   p

Shape for Front Leg Holes

Hold the first and last 7 sts on two stitch holders, leaving the remaining forty-one stitches on your main knitting needle to be worked as follows:

Row 29   k2 tog, k37, k2 tog
Row 30   p2 tog, p35, p2 tog
Row 31   k2 tog, k33, k2 tog

Row 32	p
Row 33	k
Row 34	p
Row 35	k

m1 at beg and end, including these, work as follows:

| Row 36 | p | (37 sts) |

m1 at beg and end, including these, work as follows:

| Row 37 | k | (39 sts) |

m1 at beg and end, including these, work as follows:

| Row 38 | p | (41 sts) |

Hold this work on the needle, and working first on the rs 7 sts on our stitch holder, place these 7 sts on to a 4 mm knitting needle. Work rows as follows:

Row 29	k5, k2 tog
Row 30	p2 tog, p4
Row 31	k3, k2 tog
Row 32	p
Row 33	k
Row 34	p
Row 35	k
Row 36	m1 at beg in p,	(5 sts)
Row 37	m1 at end in k,	(6 sts)
Row 38	m1 at beg in p,	(7 sts)

Place back on to stitch holder.

Now we will work the other 7 sts, working rs.

Row 29	k2 tog, k5
Row 30	p4, p2 tog
Row 31	k2 tog, k3
Row 32	p
Row 33	k
Row 34	p
Row 35	k
Row 36	m1 at end in p	(5 sts)
Row 37	m1 at beg in k	(6 sts)
Row 38	m1 at end in p	(7 sts)

Join all three parts together, totalling 55 sts.

Row 39	k
Row 40	p

Repeat rows 25 and 26 for six more rows.

Row 47	k1, *k5, k2 tog, *r, k1
Row 48	p
Row 49	*k5, k2 tog, *r, k1
Row 50	p

Change to 3¼ mm knitting needles.

Ribbing

Row 1	k1, p1
Row 2	p1, k1

Repeat rows 1 and 2 four more times.

b/o, leave enough yarn to sew the sweater together.

Medium Sleeves

On 3¼ mm knitting needles, c/o 20 sts.

Row 1	*k1, p1, *r
Row 2	*k1, p1, *r

Change to 4 mm knitting needles.

Row 3	k
Row 4	p
Row 5	k
Row 6	p
Row 7	k m1 at beg and end
Row 8	p
Row 9	k m1 at beg and end
Row 10	p

b/o

Bee Mine . . .

This sweater will be eight inches in length.

Items you will need:

3¼ mm knitting needles
4 mm knitting needles
Googly eyes
30 gm double knit yarn, four colours
Threading yarn needle
Scissors
Pencil and paper

C/o 44 sts 3¼ mm knitting needles mc.

Ribbing

Row 1   k2, p2
Row 2   k2, p2
           r for four more rows.

Change to 4 mm knitting needles.

Row 7   (rs) k

Row 8   (ws) p

             r rows 7 and 8 two more times.

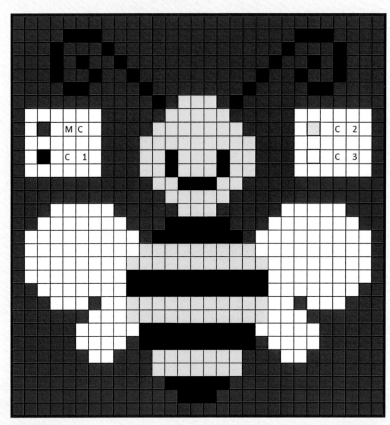

             m1, including this, work as follows:

Row 11   k21 mc, k3c1, k21 mc

Row 12   p20 mc, p5c1, p20 mc

Row 13   k19 mc, k7c2, k19 mc

Row 14   p14 mc, p2c3, p3 mc, p7c2, p3 mc, p2c3, p14 mc

             m5 sts, including these, work as follows:

Row 15   k18 mc, k4c3, k1 mc, k9c1, k1 mc, k4c3, k13 mc

             m5 sts, including these, work as follows:

Row 16   p18 mc, p5c3, p9c1, p5c3, p18 mc

Row 17   k19 mc, k3c3, k11c2, k3c3, k19 mc

Row 18   p16 mc, p3c3, p1 mc, p2c3, p11c2, p2c3, p1 mc, p3c3, p16 mc

Row 19   k15 mc, k7c3, k11c1, k7c3, k15 mc

Row 20   p14 mc, p8c3, p11c1, p8c3, p14 mc

Row 21   k14 mc, k8c3, k11c2, k8c3, k14 mc

Row 22   p14 mc, p9c3, p9c2, p9c3, p14 mc

Row 23   k14 mc, k9c3, k1 mc, k7c1, k1 mc, k9c3, k14 mc

Row 24	p15 mc, p7c3, p3 mc, p5c1, p3 mc, p7c3, p15 mc
Row 25	k16 mc, k5c3, k5 mc, k3c2, k5 mc, k5c3, k16 mc
Row 26	p25 mc, p5c2, p25 mc
Row 27	k24 mc, k2c2, k3c1, k2c2, k24 mc
Row 28	p23 mc, p2c2, p1c1, p3c2, p1c1, p2c2, p23 mc

Shape for Front Leg Holes

Hold the first and last 7 sts on two stitch holders, leaving the remaining 41 sts on your main knitting needle to be worked as follows:

Row 29	k2 togmc, k14 mc, k2c2, k1c1, k3c2, k1c1, k2c2, k14 mc, k2 togmc
Row 30	p2 togmc, p13 mc, p9c2, p13 mc, p2 togmc
Row 31	k2 togmc, k13 mc, k7c2, k13 mc, k2 togmc
Row 32	p15 mc, p5c2, p15 mc
Row 33	k14 mc, k1c1, k1 mc, k3c2, k1 mc, k1c1, k14 mc
Row 34	p7 mc, p2c1, p4 mc, p1c1, p7 mc, p1c1, p4 mc, p2c1, p7 mc
Row 35	k6 mc, k1c1, k2 mc, k1c1, k2 mc, k1c1, k9 mc, k1c1, k2 mc, k1c1, k2 mc, k1c1, k6 mc
	m1 at beg and end, including these, work as follows:
Row 36	p7 mc, p1c1, p1 mc, p1c1, p2 mc, p1c1, p11 mc, p1c1, p2 mc, p1c1, p1 mc, p1c1, p7 mc (37 sts)
	m1 at beg and end, including these, work as follows:
Row 37	k8 mc, k1c1, k3 mc, k1c1, k13 mc, k1c1, k3 mc, k1c1, k8 mc (39 sts)
	m1 at beg and end, including these, work as follows:
Row 38	p10 mc, p3c1, p15 mc, p3c1, p10 mc (41 sts)

Hold this work on the needle, and working first on the rs 7 sts on the stitch holder, place these 7 sts on to a 4 mm knitting needle. Work rows as follows:

Row 29	k5, k2 tog	
Row 30	p2 tog, p4	
Row 31	k3, k2 tog	
Row 32	p	
Row 33	k	
Row 34	p	
Row 35	k	
Row 36	m1 at beg in p	(5 sts)
Row 37	m1 at end in k	(6 sts)
Row 38	m1 at beg in p	(7 sts)

Place back on to stitch holder.

Now we will work the other 7 sts, working rs.

Row 29	k2 tog, k5
Row 30	p4, p2 tog
Row 31	k2 tog, k3
Row 32	p
Row 33	k
Row 34	p
Row 35	k
Row 36	m1 at end in p	(5 sts)
Row 37	m1 at beg in k	(6 sts)
Row 38	m1 at end in p	(7 sts)

Join all three parts together, totalling 55 sts.

Row 39	k
Row 40	p

Repeat rows 39 and 40 for six more rows.

Row 47	k1, *k5, k2 tog, *r, k1
Row 48	p
Row 49	*k5, k2 tog, *r, k1
Row 50	p2 tog, p

Change to 3¼ mm knitting needles.

Ribbing

Row 1	k2, p2
Row 2	k2, p2

Repeat rows 1 and 2 four more times.

B/o, leaving enough yarn to sew the sweater together.

Medium Sleeves

On 3¼ mm knitting needles, c/o 20 sts.

Row 1	*k1, p1, *r
Row 2	*k1, p1, *r

Change to 4 mm knitting needles.

Row 3   k
Row 4   p
Row 5   k
Row 6   p
Row 7   in k increase first and last st
Row 8   p
Row 9   in k increase first and last st
Row 10   p

b/o

Toy Ball

Items you will need:

4 mm knitting needles
15 gm double knit yarn
Threading yarn needle
Scissors
Toy filling
Pencil and paper

C/o 10 sts.

We will be doing this ball in garter st.

Row 1	k 10 sts	
Row 2	* k2 Increase 1 st *r	(14 sts)
Row 3	k	
	Repeat Row 3 two more times.	
Row 6	* k2 Increase 1 st *r	(20 sts)
Row 7	k	
	Repeat Row 7 two more times.	

Row 10	* k3 Increase 1 st *r	(26 sts)
Row 11	k	
	Repeat Row 11 five more times.	
Row 17	*k3, k2 tog, *r, k1	(21 sts)
Row 18	k	
	Repeat Row 18 two more times.	
Row 21	*k2, k2 tog, *r, k1	(16 sts)
Row 22	k	
	Repeat Row 22 two more times.	
Row 25	*k2, k2 tog, *r	(12 sts)
Row 26	*k2, k2 tog, *r	(9 sts)
Row 27	k2, k2 tog, s1, k1, psso, k1, k2 tog	(6 sts)
Row 28	*k1, k2 tog, *r	(4 sts)
Row 29	k2 tog, k2 tog	

b/o   leave enough yarn to sew the ball up.

Assembling the Ball

Working with the ball ws out, begin to sew the ball together. When you have approximately an inch left, turn the ball rs out and begin to fill. Once you have the ball nice and full, sew the remaining hole up. Like with the other knitted toys, take your yarn needle with the yarn still attached, and thread from one side all the way through to the other side. With tension, hold yarn and cut. The yarn end will disappear into the ball, leaving no unsightly ends.

Roll in the palm of your hands to achieve the roundness and shape.

Pom-pom Hat

4″ wide (x-small)

Items you will need:

3¼ mm knitting needles
15 gm double knit yarn
Threading yarn needle
Scissors
Pom-pom
Sewing needle
Cotton thread
Pencil and paper

On 3¼ mm knitting needles, c/o 36 sts.

Garter st for four rows.

Row 1	k
Row 2	k
	Repeat rows 1 and 2 two more times.

Now in stst.

Row 5	k
Row 6	k4, p28, k4

R these rows 5 and 6 for sixteen more rows.

b/o, leaving approximately 7" of yarn to sew the hat together.

Now fold in half, and with the 7" of yarn, sew along the b/o row.

Once you have sewn up and are in the corner point of the hat, thread the yarn through to the outer side of the hat and attach the pom-pom. Secure and cut excess yarn.

Tassels

Now cut ten pieces of 24" yarn, and two pieces of 12" yarn. Thread the 12" yarn through the corner of the hat, leaving most yarn through. Tie off and leave. Now thread the five pieces of the 24" piece one at a time into the same area. This yarn we want to pull through so that it has approximately 12" each side and tie to secure. Divide the yarn into three double strands and plait. Do a simple knot to hold the end of the plait together. Now beneath the knot, trim yarn tassel threads to tidy.

Paw Hat

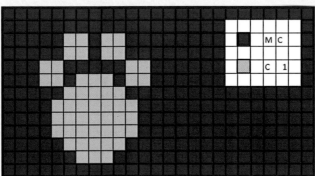

5″ wide (small)

Items you will need:

4 mm knitting needles
20 gm chunky knit yarn
Pom-pom
Threading yarn needle
Scissors

Pencil and paper

On 4 mm knitting needles in c1, c/o 35 sts.

Row 1	*k1, p1, *r
	Repeat Row 1 three more times.
	Change to mc.

Row 5	k
Row 6	p
Row 7	k16 mc, k3c1, k16 mc
Row 8	p15 mc, p5c1, p15 mc
Row 9	k14 mc, k7c1, k14 mc
Row 10	p14 mc, p7c1, p14 mc
Row 11	k14 mc, k7c1, k14 mc
Row 12	p15 mc, p5c1, p15 mc
Row 13	k13 mc, k2c1, k1 mc, k3c1, k1 mc, k2c1, k13 mc
Row 14	p13 mc, p2c1, p5 mc, p2c1
Row 15	k15 mc, k2c1, k1 mc, k2c1, k15 mc
Row 16	p15 mc, p2c1, p1 mc, p2c1, p15 mc
Row 17	k

| Row 18 | p |
| | R rows 17 and 18 four more times. |

b/o, leaving approximately 7" of yarn to sew the hat together.

Now fold in half, and with the 7" of yarn, sew along the b/o row.

Once you have sewn up and are in the corner point of the hat, thread the yarn through to the outer side of the hat and attach the pom-pom. Secure and cut excess yarn.

Tassels

Now cut two pieces of 24" yarn c1 and two pieces of 12" yarn mc. Thread one of the 12" yarn through the corner of the hat, leaving most yarn through. Tie off and leave. Now thread one piece of 24" yarn into the same area. This yarn we want to pull through so that it has approximately 12" each side and tie to secure. Now take the three strands and plait. Do a simple knot to hold the end of the plait together. Now beneath the knot, trim yarn tassel threads to tidy.

Abbreviations

c/o	cast on
sts	stitches
st	stitch
stst	stocking stitch
k	knit
p	purl
k2 tog	knit two together
rs	right side
ws	wrong side
s1	slip 1 stitch
psso	pass slip stitch over
b/o	bind off
rpt	repeat
r	repeat
m1	make 1
m5	make 5
beg	beginning
mc	main colour
c1	colour 1
c2	colour 2
c3	colour 3
c4	colour 4

Edwards Brothers Malloy
Oxnard, CA USA
January 26, 2015